A PLACE TO BELONG

BRENDA CRISSMAN MUSICK

Jan-Carol
Publishing, Inc

A PLACE TO BELONG

BRENDA CRISSMAN MUSICK

Published November 2014
Little Creek Books
Imprint of Jan-Carol Publishing, Inc.
All rights reserved
Copyright © Brenda Crissman Musick

ISBN: 978-1-939289-51-3
Library of Congress Control Number: 2014956321

You may contact the publisher:
Jan-Carol Publishing, Inc.
PO Box 701 Johnson City, TN 37605
publisher@jancarolpublishing.com
jancarolpublishing.com

Dedicated to:

My Parents,

Clarence and Mamie Stump Crissman

...who taught me the priorities of life:

God-First

Family-Second

Others-Third

Beloved, let us love one another, for love is of God;

and everyone that loveth is born of God, and knoweth God.

1 John 4:7

And also to:

My Maternal Grandparents

Thomas and Caroline Ray Stump

...whose lives were the inspiration

for the Trials of an Appalachian Family duo:

One-Eyed Tom and A Place to Belong.

In thee, O Lord, do I put my trust.

Psalm 31:1

ACKNOWLEDGEMENTS

So many people have influenced the writing of this book and I am grateful to each one. My mother has passed away since the writing of *One-Eyed Tom*, but I was able to sit by her bedside and read the novel to her before she died. Much of it and this novel, *A Place to Belong*, were born from stories she told me. Her mind was alert even unto her last days. What a legacy she has left to me!

My childhood contributed to this writing, as I grew up in these hills of Appalachia, enjoying the beauty of its nature and participating in the love, friendship and closeness of its people. There is no place on earth I would rather be. I like the front porch socialization, the "howdys" from neighbors and knowing any one of them would be there to help in a crisis at a moment's notice.

There are no words adequate to describe the contribution my husband has made to my work. He is my encourager, my editor, my helper. He is the only one I allow to read my manuscript before it goes to the publisher, so he retires to his little "John Deere room" to read so I won't see him cry. He never begrudges my time at the computer while my house grows dusty from lack of care and meals often consist of a bologna sandwich. His first words after reading my manuscript are, "Have you started the next book yet?"

I owe much to my brother Jim and his wife Mary, who constantly encourage me. Jim is all I have left of my childhood family, and we had a memorable childhood together, playing cowboys and Indians, wading creeks and riding bikes. I was Annie Oakley and he was Wild Bill Hickok...or Gene Autry...or Johnny Mack Brown. His memory has also added to my books.

I also owe gratitude to my two support groups: my Reminiscent Writers Group of Southwest Virginia Community College and to my church family at Swords Creek Community Baptist Church. They never fail me.

Most of all, I owe everything I am and any capability I have to God. He has so richly blessed me and brought me through the hard times, giving me strength when I had none.

LETTER FROM THE AUTHOR

Dear Reader,

The split apple tree on the cover of this book once stood on my husband's boyhood farm, the farm on which we now live. It was just an ordinary apple tree, producing small apples good for making applesauce and apple butter. Then one day a storm came. The thunder roared and the lightning flashed. The lightning suddenly hit the little apple tree, splitting it down the middle almost to the ground, but the little apple tree didn't fall. It never produced apples again and, seemingly, served no useful purpose, yet it continued to stand and my father-in-law refused to cut it down.

Our lives are sometimes like the split apple tree. They are split, maybe broken, but we don't have to fall. We can refuse to let life's tragedies cut us down. With God's help, we can stand tall and we can serve a purpose. It may be different from our purpose before the tragedy, but we can still serve in some capacity. None of us are without a purpose. We sometimes must bend with the storms and then look up.

You see, the purpose of the little apple tree changed. It produced no more apples, but it stood as an example. It was often a conversation piece... and it made it to the cover of this book when no other apple tree was worthy. We are all unique and important...and we all have *a place to belong*.

INTRODUCTION

BY: DORIS MUSICK,
AUTHOR AND PUBLISHER

When Brenda Crissman Musick began the first in a series, *One-Eyed Tom*, she began her story with an old Appalachian tradition: a corn shucking and storytelling. Musick herself was privy to many of these old stories through both her mother and father, and she has remained faithful to that tradition and to the manner in which the stories were related.

The chronicle of the Ranes and Swank families is too explosive for only one book, and our story continues in the second in the series, *A Place to Belong*. Musick has a clear understanding of the hardships endured by these mountain folk and she tells us their story with clarity and compassion. We are sometimes on a roller coaster ride, torn between sympathy and accusations; between praise and condemnation. But whatever our feelings toward each of the characters, we are never bored.

For those who have read *One-Eyed Tom*, you were left wanting more and Musick has adequately provided us with the rest of the story in *A Place to Belong*. A must read, so sit back and be prepared to enjoy!

A COUNTRY BOY'S PLIGHT

Sadness envelopes his being,
As the memories plummet down.
Today he's returning to his roots,
To his Appalachian boyhood town.

A plethora of thoughts quickly greet him,
Swirling unchecked through his head.
Life abounds wherever he looks,
But inside, he feels so dead.

He's been running from the memories,
Trying hard to ease the pain.
He's traveled far, labored long,
But the running has been in vain.

Here is where he found her...
The beautiful joy of his life.
Yet, here is where he lost it all.
She could never be his wife.

He's spent years now searching,
His yearning for peace so strong.
Please grant him a bit of happiness, Lord,
And a simple place to belong.

– Brenda Crissman Musick

CHAPTER 1

Eight years ... eight whole years since he had been home. The thoughts and memories chased each other relentlessly around in his head as Luke disembarked from the train. It had been a long, dusty train ride from Pennsylvania, but he was finally here. He stood at the bottom of the last step, looking around, searching for something familiar. The old train depot seemed the same, yet different, older and rundown. The white paint on the building was now yellowed with age and crumbled as he ran his finger down the side. Looking at the flakes on his fingers, he thought, *That's how I feel ... old and rundown ... withered ... crumbled....* Yet he knew at twenty-nine he could be neither. Maybe it was just his heart that was old, rundown and crumbled. It was certainly empty. Outside the depot he watched for a moment as several men sat on kegs around an old wooden table, playing some sort of card game.

Walking on toward the little town of Haymaker in the cool early May air, Luke saw familiar sights. There was the old mill where Paw came to have their corn ground. It still seemed to be in running order. *I wonder if Mr. Gardner still runs it,* he thought. *No. Why he must be nigh on ninety years old now, if he's still living. Maybe his son Grover took it over.* Just beyond the mill and a few other buildings was Haymaker Hotel. Oh, the memories the sight of it stirred in him. *Alice worked there. We were supposed to have been married there. My Alice. She'll always be My Alice. I know she's married, and I hope she's happy, but I'll always think of her as My Alice ... my beautiful, sweet Alice.*

Luke shook his head to dislodge the cobweb of tangled thoughts, then continued walking. He paused to watch two robins flying to and from a cherry tree, carrying the makings for a nest, first the female then the male, working together. *Even the birds have someone,* he thought.

Before he knew it, he stood in front of Berke's Mercantile, and he couldn't help but smile. Oh, how many times he had been there. As a little boy he had loved to go in and buy a licorice stick. He knew from Maw's letters that Mr. Faller had retired two or three years ago, but she had not said who ran it now. He decided to go in, and as he opened the door, a small bell gave a jingle. *That's certainly new,* he mused, *but a nice, homey touch.*

"Good morning!" called a cheerful, feminine voice. Unable to see the source of that voice, he walked toward the counter. There stood one of the loveliest sights he had seen in ages. He guessed her to be about twenty or so, and she had the most beautiful dancing blue eyes. They matched her long blonde hair, cascading in glistening waves almost to her waist. Luke realized he was staring and cleared his throat to bring himself together.

"I don't believe I've seen you in here before," said Blue Eyes. "May I help you with something?"

The sound of her voice reminds me of a happy song. Luke cleared his throat again. "No, ma'am. I mean, I don't exactly know." His face was, by now, the color of a ripe tomato.

"My name is Mandy Faller," she said, sensing his discomfort. "Actually it's Amanda, but no one has called me that in a long time."

"I'm Luke Swank," he finally managed. "I've been away for a few years and just wanted to come in and see the old place. Mr. Faller use to be the manager and he was good to me, as he was to everyone. Always took time to make me feel important, even though I just came in to buy a licorice stick. Mmm! I can still taste those licorice sticks! Faller? Did you say your last name is Faller? I didn't think the Fallers had children."

"The Fallers are my aunt and uncle," explained Mandy, as a distant look shadowed her eyes. "My parents died a year ago and I moved here to live with them. I was given a job here by the owner and now I'm the manager."

Luke continued to stare. "I'm so sorry about your parents. Was it an accident, if you don't mind me asking?"

Her eyes suddenly became sad, and Luke regretted asking such a personal question. "No, it was no accident. There was a diphtheria outbreak over in Kentucky where we lived. Poppa died first and Mama followed three days later. For some reason I never came down with it. I suppose God has a purpose for me here yet, and I hope I can fulfill that purpose. Did you say your last name is Swank? I know a Jessie Swank and Miss Carrie, his mother, as well as the girls, Belinda, Ady Rose and Cindy. They are all such good folks. You must be the long-lost brother I've heard about."

"Jessie's my younger brother," smiled Luke. "I've been away for the past eight years, working with the sawmills in Pennsylvania and Brazil."

Mandy's eyes grew large. "Brazil! Wow! That's so far away, although I've read about it. I can't believe I'm talking to someone who has been to Brazil. I'd love to hear all about it."

"Well, sometime I'd love to tell you about it," replied Luke, suddenly feeling a little lighter in spirit, "but right now I'd better be heading toward home. Maw doesn't even know I'm coming."

"I know she'll be happy to see you," said Mandy. "Miss Carrie is such a fine woman. Tell her hello for me. Oh, wait just a minute."

With this she disappeared. Quickly she returned, smiling and holding out a licorice stick to Luke. "Here. This is a gift for old time's sake and it's on the house."

Accepting the gift, Luke smiled and said with a bow, "Much obliged, ma'am."

As he turned to go, Mandy called to him, "Tell Jessie hello for me!"

Continuing on his way, Luke's thoughts were filled with Mandy. *Was there some underlying meaning when she mentioned saying hello to Jessie. Her expression seemed to change when she said his name. Does my little brother have a girlfriend?*

Walking on, he passed the little house where he and Alice had planned to live. He felt as though a knife had pierced his heart and was twisting and twisting relentlessly. Belinda and Joe lived there now, but he couldn't stop ... couldn't make himself go inside that house where he was supposed to have been so happy. He started to move on when something caught his eye. Something white. Could it be? Yes. It was the snowball bush Alice had planted the day they had bought the house. Why, it was all of five feet tall now and beautiful, just like Alice. Memories attacked Luke with a vengeance. He remembered Alice's excitement as she had planned where each piece of furniture would go ... her sparkling brown eyes as she flitted from room to room.

Right here, Luke, she had trilled. *We'll place our little table and chairs here, and I'll cook for you every night. I'll fix your favorite meals. Oh Luke, I do so love the coziness of eating right in the kitchen with all the wonderful smells. Don't you think it's better than an old dining room?*

Luke had laughed out loud, reveling in her enthusiasm. Oh, the memories ... until Paw and Lily had ruined it all. Reluctantly pulling himself from the past, he continued his journey, seeing familiar homes and landmarks. Up the road a ways he saw the place where he and Belinda used to pick blackberries. Maw made the best blackberry pies in the whole world, not to mention her blackberry jam and blackberry dumplings. His mouth watered just remembering. Little had changed, and yet, everything had changed. Alice wasn't there. His paw was dead ... not that Luke missed him or his cruelty and the misery that came with him. Never had he shed a tear for the man, but many for the pain he had caused the family.

"Luke! Luke Swank, is that you?" he heard a voice calling.

Turning, he immediately recognized the face. It was Ady Rose's husband Willy. "Yes, it's me and none other. How are you, Willy? Is my sister treating you well?" With this he gave him a firm handshake and then drew him into a hug.

"No," answered Willy, a look of pain distorting his face. "I'm afraid she treats me poorly, Luke. See how I'm wasting away. Maybe now that you're home you can talk to her about this cruelty."

Luke laughed, almost surprised that he still knew how. "You don't look like you've missed too many meals, my boy!" With this, he slapped Willy on the back and they both enjoyed a laugh.

Then Willy became serious. "Does your maw know you're coming Luke? She hasn't said a word to us."

"No. This is a complete surprise," he replied, shaking his head. "I just returned from Brazil two weeks ago, handed in my resignation at the sawmill in Lewistown, and headed this way. I just had a hankering for home and family. Don't know what I'll do for a living, but I'll find something."

"They will all be overjoyed to see you," Willy said. "Maw Carrie has missed you something fierce, and I can't begin to tell you how exited Ady Rose will be when I tell her."

Luke smiled. "I'd best be getting on before it gets late. Maw might lock me out. Tell Ady Rose I'm looking forward to seeing her ... and talking to her about starving her fine husband to the point of death."

Within a few minutes Luke was in sight of the tall water tank where he had watched in awe so many times as the old steam engine had stopped and filled up with water. He could remember the engineer pulling the rope so the water trough was just over the space for filling the engine's tank. He could see the water running through the trough. When the tank was full, the engineer returned the trough to its former position. As a child, he had been mesmerized each time he watched. Pulling his eyes away from the water tank, he looked to the hill above. There was his home! There was the house where he grew up...where he learned about love from his dear sweet mother, but where he also learned to hate his cruel, unfaithful father. He remembered the day he received the news that his father was found dead, lying face down in the river. He had felt no grief, no sadness ... just utter relief. *I was just relieved,* he admitted to himself, *that he could no longer hurt Maw or any of us children. He's the reason I lost My Alice.*

Shaking his head to erase the thoughts, Luke headed on up the hill, his steps just a little jauntier. He was on his way to see Maw! He had thought of this moment constantly for the past two weeks, and now he could wait no longer. Nearing the gate, he saw her. She was sitting in her old rocking chair on the front porch, and as he drew closer, he could see that she was asleep. Reaching the top of the steps, he paused, just drinking in the sight of her ... his dear, dear mother. Oh, how he loved her! She looked older. Gray had begun to mingle with her beautiful black hair, and yet her face, now with fine wrinkles around her eyes and mouth, still had that softness. He remembered that softness ... the love in her eyes and in her voice. She was holding her Bible in her lap, and Luke knew she had fallen asleep reading it. He could just imagine one of the scriptures she had been reading. *For I know that my redeemer liveth, and that he shall stand at the latter*

5

day upon the earth; and though after my skin worms destroy this body, yet my flesh shall see God....

Luke was amazed that he could still remember the verse. He hadn't been much for reading the Bible in the past eight years. The verse was from the book of Job, but he couldn't remember exactly where. Maw had made them memorize it and many others. He smiled to himself as he thought about saying that verse and imagining worms crawling all over his body. He never told Maw about that. He knelt down beside her rocker and placed his hand on hers. "Maw," he whispered gently. "Maw, are you awake?"

As Carrie roused from her sleep, she looked at him. Then her eyes grew round with surprise. "Luke, is that you? Oh Lord, please don't let me be dreaming!" she cried.

Luke laughed softly. "You're not dreaming, Maw. It's really me. Oh, it's so good to see you, my darling mother." With this he put his arms around her and his head on her shoulder just as he had done innumerable times as a child. Her shoulder was a place of shelter and love when everything around him was in turmoil. She pulled him tightly to her, and he could feel her tears dampening his own face. Maw had always been this way ... always loving and never hesitant to show it.

"My dear boy," she said, still holding him tightly. "I have longed for the day I would see you again, yet at the same time, afraid that it might never be."

Sitting up straight in her chair, she pushed him back, ever so gently. "Let me get a look at you. My, you've grown so strong and handsome. You have the look of your grandpa Silas, but taller and even more handsome."

He laughed again. "I will take that as the greatest of compliments. Maw, how have you been? I can't wait to hear all the news and just sit and talk with you. We have so much catching up to do. I have truly missed you these eight years I've been away."

Carrie smiled, and Luke just wanted to hold on to that smile forever. "Are you here to stay for awhile, Luke? You don't have to hurry back to Pennsylvania do you?"

He held her hand in his. "I have plenty of time, Maw. How does forever sound?"

"What do you mean?" she gasped, the hope ripe in her eyes.

"I'm home to stay," whispered Luke. "I'm not going back to Pennsylvania. I'm tired of being alone. Don't know what kind of work I'll find here, but anything will do as long as I can be near my family."

"Oh, praise God!" said Carrie. "Praise my dear Lord! Those are the happiest words I have heard in a long, long time."

At this point, they were interrupted by another voice. "Maw, do you know where I put that stack of papers I brought home last night? I thought I put them on...."

And the voice stopped abruptly as Jessie stood just inside the screen door, his mouth gaping. Then the door flew open and his arms were around Luke, tears streaming down his tanned cheeks.

"Brother, oh Brother!" was all he could say, for both were crying uncontrollably. Carrie beamed as she watched the two, who had always been so close, knowing the bond between them was a special one.

Finally, gaining some control, Jessie pushed back from Luke. "Well, it's about time you got back home, you sorry rascal! We thought you'd forgotten all about us country folk."

Carrie could restrain herself no longer. "He's home to stay, Jessie! He just told me!"

"Well, I do declare," laughed Jessie. "Finally realized where you belong, didn't you?"

"Guess you could say that," replied Luke, an unsolicited cloud shading his jubilant spirit. "I guess a man can travel the world over, but if he don't have family, then he don't have anything. Took me a while to realize that, but here I am."

"And we are thankful for that," said Maw. "We are certainly thankful for that."

With this, she took the hand of each son and smiled up at them with the joy and love that can shine only in a mother's eyes.

CHAPTER 2

Carrie insisted on fixing supper for her boys, and after enjoying the best meal Luke had eaten in years, the three of them sat and talked more. A long-forgotten peace slowly wrapped its arms around Luke and he knew, without a doubt, coming home was the right decision.

"Tell me about everyone," urged Luke. "I'm so hungry to hear the news and to see Belinda and Ady Rose and Cindy. What about Clay? When is he coming home?"

Jessie laughed, "One question at a time, big brother! One at a time!"

Sighing, Luke said, "Okay. Well, first, how is Belinda? I know she longs for a baby. No luck there?"

Carrie's eyes clouded with sadness. "The doctors have told her she will never be able to have a child, Luke. That's been hard for her to accept, and we really feared for her health and sanity for awhile, but staying busy has helped. Cindy works with her part time, and you know your baby sister. She just has a way of seeing the good in life and cheering up the most forlorn."

"Life really hands us some hard knocks sometimes," said Luke, shaking his head. "Seems to me Belinda was just cut out to be a mother."

"I haven't given up," responded Carrie. "With God, all things are possible."

"Speaking of my baby sister," continued Luke, "I'll bet she has boy-friends fighting over her if she's as pretty as she was eight years ago."

Jessie laughed. "Oh she's even prettier, and yes, she can have any boy she wants. All she has to do is bat those gorgeous blue eyes and they come a-running."

Carrie picked up with his sentence. "But she doesn't want a boyfriend. That's the thing of it. Cindy wants to be a school teacher and she has her mind set on it. Right now she works part time at the school with Darla Cross, but someday I know she'll have a school of her own."

"The sad part for Maw, though," interjected Jessie, "is that for Cindy to fulfill her dream, she will have to move away, and that will nigh on break Maw's heart."

"I reckon it will at that," Carrie smiled weakly. "But my children must do what they must. I want them to be happy and use the gifts God has given them. I had to say goodbye to Luke and then to Clay, but just look ... one is back to stay."

Luke smiled lovingly at his maw. "What about Ady Rose? Tell me about her and Willy and those two young'uns you always write about. By the way, I saw Willy as I was on my way here."

Carrie smiled contentedly. "Ady Rose is just happy being a wife and mother...and a good one she is, at that. Those two little darlings are a full-time job, too."

"Is Belinda at the hotel full time?" Luke questioned.

"She is now manager of the Haymaker Hotel," answered Carrie. "Mrs. Faller had to retire to take care of her husband, who had a stroke a couple of years back. I think I mentioned it in one of my letters. She made Belinda the manager then, and things are going quite well. Like I said, Cindy helps her on the days she isn't working at the school, and Belinda recently hired a new girl, Syrena Blackburn, to help her. You'll like Syrena, Luke. She is from over in Kentucky, near where my sister Ellie lives. As a matter of fact, it was Ellie who introduced Syrena to us in a letter."

"She's not a bit bad to look at either, Brother," added Jessie, giving Luke a poke in the ribs.

"Oh, and Mr. and Mrs. Faller's niece moved here from Kentucky and is now running Berke's Mercantile," continued Carrie, ignoring Jessie's good-natured banter.

Luke smiled. "As a matter of fact, I met the lovely Mandy earlier. I stopped by Berke's Mercantile just to see if it had changed, and there stood one of the loveliest creatures I have ever seen. By the way, that lovely creature told me to say hello to you, Jessie. Is there something I should know about, brother? Has an old scruff of a fellow like you got that magnificent damsel fooled?"

Jessie could not hide the sudden crimson that came to his cheeks. "Not a thing you should know about, big brother, and don't get started on me and women. As I've told you many times over, I ain't never getting married."

Luke caught the sudden pained expression in his mother's eyes and decided to change the subject. "How old are Ady Rose and Willy's children now, Maw?"

The smile immediately returned to Carrie's face, and Luke could see the love there as she answered, "Leah is almost eight, looks just like her mother, and is sharp as a tack. Nathan is four, looks like Joe, and is the sweetest rascal you will ever meet. They keep Ady Rose on her toes, and needless to say, I adore both of them."

"And how about my baby brother?" questioned Luke. "Is Clay enjoying his life on the horse ranch? And what's this you've been writing about a girl in his life?"

"Our baby brother is quite smitten," laughed Jessie, before Maw could answer, "with the horses and Miss Abigail McCleary. Not sure which ranks first. I don't think Clay will ever be coming back home to live, but he's been hinting that he may be coming for a visit soon and bringing the lovely Miss Abigail with him."

Maw nodded in agreement. "I do believe Clay is more than fond of this young lady, Luke, and I'm hoping he'll bring her home to meet us. His letters are filled with happiness and excitement, so what more could I ask for?"

"At least one of the Swank boys may find love and happiness," said Luke, a cloud of despair enveloping his face. "Speaking of love and happiness, what have you heard from Alice and her husband lately?"

For a moment silence pervaded the living room as Carrie and Jessie exchanged a nervous glance. Then Carrie spoke. "I didn't want to tell you this in a letter, son, but Alice's husband died a few months ago."

Luke's face became ashen. "Oh no, Maw. I must confess I have often begrudged her happiness with another man, but I would never wish this on her. I always wanted her happiness above all else. What happened?"

Carrie patted her son's hand. "Her husband Walter was some twenty years her senior. I don't know if I told you that or not. She knew when she married him that he had a very weak heart, and in the past year he grew steadily worse, until he was bedfast. Alice took care of him day and night, but his heart just gave out."

"What will she do now?" asked Luke.

"He left her enough money for the funeral expenses," replied Carrie, "but she's back working at the hotel where she worked when she first left here. Her letters sound happy enough, but I can read between the lines. That darling girl has had more than her share of heartaches. She lost a child about two years after they married ... a little girl ... just six months old. Alice put her to bed one night, and when she checked on her later, she was cold and lifeless. I can only imagine the pain. I've had my share of troubles and heartaches, but nothing to compare to losing a child."

Luke sat in silence, empty of words. *My Alice*, he thought. *My poor, darling Alice.*

The silence was finally broken by the sound of an excited feminine voice. "Where is he? Where is my big brother? I know he's here, so don't try to fool me."

Cindy bounced into the room and threw herself into Luke's waiting arms. "Oh Luke, it is so very good to see you. Why on earth did you stay away so long? My, you're so tall ... and good looking ... but don't let that swell your head! How long are you going to stay? At least two weeks? Tell me you'll stay two weeks, Luke. We have so much to catch up on."

With this, Luke burst into laughter. "Hey, girl, one question at a time. I must say, though, you do know how to make a fellow feel welcome. Let me look at you. Well, you don't look too bad for an old spinster."

"Bite your tongue," she responded, hitting him playfully on the shoulder. "I am no ways near to being a spinster...although I will be, because I

11

never plan to marry. I'm going to be a school teacher. Now answer me ... how long can you stay with us?"

"He's not going to leave us, Cindy," laughed her mother. "Luke is home to stay!"

This news brought another squeal and hug from Cindy. "Oh, I can't wait for us to catch up on the past eight years. Tell me everything, Luke, especially about Brazil. I want to tell my students about it. Hey, maybe you could come to the school one day and talk to them!"

The four of them talked well into the night as Luke answered their questions and caught up on family news and the goings-on in Haymaker. When they finally retired to their beds, Luke fell asleep almost immediately, surrounded by familiar things and a peace that had eluded him for a long, long time.

CHAPTER 3

He awoke the next morning to the aroma of fried sausage and bis-cuits. Lying in his old bed, staring up at the ceiling, he slowly smiled to himself. *Home,* he thought to himself. *I'm finally home.* With this he bounded from the bed, anxious to dress and get to the kitchen. With the smell of sausage, he knew there had to be Maw's gravy, too, and she made the best gravy in the whole wide world.

As he entered the kitchen, Maw stood over the stove turning the sausage in the cast-iron frying pan. What a sight she was!

"Good morning, Maw," he said, bending down to kiss her cheek.

She responded with the beautiful smile that Luke well remembered. "Good morning, Luke. I was hoping you would get up early so I would know last night was not a dream."

"No dream, Maw," laughed Luke. "I can't wait to taste those biscuits and my Maw's famous gravy. Wow, is that fried apples I see in the bowl? With butter and cinnamon? Yum-yum! Aren't the others up yet?"

Carrie laughed. "Cindy left over an hour ago, Luke, and Jessie's out feeding the cows and chickens. We just let you have your rest, but don't go getting spoiled. There will be plenty of work for you to do to earn your keep, young man."

Laughing, Luke gave his maw a hug. "I can't wait to work on this old place again, Maw. I know I'll have to find some work, but for a few weeks I just want to get the feel of farm work again. And this time I won't have Paw criticizing every move I make."

Sadness suddenly erased the smile from Carrie's face, and Luke was immediately sorry he had mentioned his Paw. *Does she still love Paw after all he did to her and his family?* he wondered, but would not dare ask. Instead he sat down at the old table where he had eaten so many times in his life. He couldn't wait to have another of Maw's breakfasts.

"Well, did ole lazy bones finally decide to get out of bed?" Jessie's taunting voice boomed from the doorway. "Sure takes a lot of beauty sleep for some people. We'll soon get that out of him, Maw, and put a few calluses on those lily white hands."

Luke laughed warmly. "Maybe this fork will help with those calluses, because I intend to work mighty hard with it for the next several minutes. May wear me out, though, and I'll have to take a nap. Sit down here, brother, and have some breakfast."

Looking aghast, Jessie replied, "I ate breakfast hours ago. Someone has to get the work done around here. But, now that you mention it, I might just have one of those biscuits with some apple butter on it. Would it be too much work for you to pass me one, kind sir?"

Carrie laughed joyfully. "Oh, it does this old heart good to hear my boys bantering once more. Now both of you just sit and eat and talk. I'm going to put some beans on for supper."

After Jessie's third biscuit and countless ones for Luke, the boys stood and began clearing their plates from the table. The slamming of a door made them halt.

"Luke, oh Luke, where are you?" called a feminine voice that could only belong to Ady Rose. Before anyone could answer, she was through the kitchen doorway, arms firmly encircling her oldest brother, almost knocking him off balance.

"I must say, sis, you do know how to make an entrance," laughed Luke, getting a better grip on the plate in his hands. "You look absolutely radiant, girl. Willy must be treating you well."

"Don't go giving Willy credit," warned Ady Rose. "His head swells at the least little compliment. And, big brother, you don't look so bad your-

14

self. Look at those shoulders. I'll bet that's from lifting lumber, as well as swinging the girls."

Luke shook his head. "Lifting lumber, yes. Swinging girls, no. I have no place in my life for women. Speaking of Willy, and changing the subject, where is that sorry coot?"

"Oh, he and his paw are busy on the farm," she replied. "He'll be over on Sunday. He never likes to miss one of Maw's Sunday dinners."

"From the looks of him yesterday, he hasn't missed many of anyone's dinners," laughed Luke. "Willy's a good one, Ady Rose. Glad to call him my brother-in-law, but don't you dare tell him I said so. I'll go to my grave denying it."

At this moment Jessie returned from carrying his dishes to the kitchen. "Well, brother, are you going to stand around talking all day or are you going to do some actual man's work for a change? I took the day off so we could look over the farm at all the things that need a-doing ... and there are plenty. Thought we might start with some fencing. That is, if you think you're up to some real manly labor."

"I just hope you can keep up, little brother," laughed Luke, slapping Jessie on the back.

"Well, I like that," declared Ady Rose, hands on hips. "I come all the way over here to visit with my prodigal brother and all you two can think about is fencing. That's a fine how-do-you-do. I can get that much attention at home."

"You can keep your old maw company for awhile," said Carrie as she walked into the room. "These two always did have a mind of their own. Besides, we'll all be together Sunday afternoon for plenty of catching up."

With this, the brothers took their leave, heading for the old tool shed, leaving Maw and Ady Rose staring after them.

They walked in silence for a few minutes, until Jessie spoke. "I don't mean to rush you into work, Luke. I just felt you might like to get out for awhile ... do some working, thinking and remembering. Sometimes we have to face the memories before we can get on with our lives."

Luke, paused, as though pondering on Jessie's words. "I've spent eight years running from the memories, Jessie, and it took me that long to realize it was useless. Memories are a part of us, I guess. I have some wonderful memories here, and some that have given me plenty of nightmares through the years. I hope, by coming home, I can get rid of the bad stuff and remember the good."

"I don't think we'll ever get rid of the bad, Brother," said Jessie, shaking his head. "I think we just have to learn from the bad ... then maybe it won't seem so bad. Does that make any sense at all?"

"Yeah," replied Luke. "It makes sense. I'm just not sure I know how to do it. I don't know if I can ever stop hating Paw and all that he did to our lives, but the Good Book says I'm supposed to forgive. Now how do I do that, Jessie? The last memory I have of this old tool shed is Paw beating me with an old piece of horse's rein. I think he must have beaten me with every kind of whip he could come up with over the years. How can I forget that? Just tell me, Brother."

"I don't know the answer," said Jessie, shaking his head. "I haven't found a way to forgive him myself. But the worst thing, Luke, is that I'm afraid of being like him. I ain't ever gonna marry, because I'm afraid I might do the things he did, and I don't want to cause that kind of hurt. I'm better off single and lonely."

Luke put his arm around Jessie's shoulder. "You don't have any of that in you, Jessie. I can promise you that. Maybe if we work together we can rid ourselves of some of this hate and anger. I want to, because it's eating me up inside, and Paw ain't worth that. We can't let him win."

"Well, I suggest we start ridding ourselves of the anger by working on the fence around the hayfield," suggested Jessie, attempting to smile. "I can tell you this ... there's enough work around here to keep us busy for a long time. With my job as sheriff, I can't do near all that needs doing to keep this old farm in shape. I think I'm gonna like having some help."

CHAPTER 4

The week passed quickly and Sunday was upon them before they knew it. The Swanks had looked forward to this Sunday get-together for a long time. They would all be there together except for Clay. Belinda had been so busy at the hotel, she had not had a chance to come see Luke, and he couldn't bring himself to go to the hotel. A few memories at a time were all he could handle. He had become used to rising when Old Bill the rooster crowed, and he had blisters bigger than he had ever imagined. This Sunday morning he and Jessie had finished all the outside chores and were just enjoying some rest and talk as they waited for their siblings to arrive. Maw and Cindy had been in the kitchen since daylight, cooking up all kinds of great-smelling food.

The peace and tranquility were broken by the sound of children's voices. "I got here first!" declared one voice that Luke figured to be his nephew Nathan's. "I get to tell Uncle Luke hello first."

"Well, a gentleman would let a lady go first!" declared the feminine voice. "I guess you're not a gentleman."

"No, I'm not," came the reply, "and you certainly ain't no lady."

At this time, Ady Rose took over. "If I hear one more word, both of you will go back and sit beside the railroad and wait until it's time to go home, and neither of you will say hello to Uncle Luke."

"I agree with your mother on that," sounded Willy.

Jessie and Luke were rolling with laughter by this time. "Why don't both of you come give your old Uncle Luke a hug," called Luke.

At this, a beautiful young replica of Ady Rose and a rough little version of Willy flew into the room, both throwing their arms around Luke. He pulled them to him, laughing in a way he had not been able to in a long, long time.

"Now how did two good looking young'uns like these come from the likes of you two?" Luke asked.

Ady Rose laughed, coming to give Luke a hug and then one for Jessie. "I guess the Good Lord just blessed us. At least they don't look like you two scruffy things."

Before he could think of a reply, another voice called out, "Where is my long lost brother?"

Luke jumped to his feet and headed to the door. There stood Belinda, his dear sister ... the one he had protected and cared for, no matter what the circumstances. Just looking at her brought back memories. There was the time she almost died. Oh, how he had prayed as he sat beside her bed. There was the time he had gotten in a fight at school because some boys were taunting her about being old One-Eyed Tom's daughter. Now, here she stood, a beautiful young woman, looking more like Maw than he could ever have imagined. Luke opened the screen door and drew her into his arms.

"Beanie, you're just a sight for sore eyes," he declared. "I have truly missed you."

"And I have missed you, my big brother," she laughed. "It's about time you came home where you belong."

Luke smiled at her words. *I hope that's true,* he thought. *I need so desperately to belong somewhere ... to have purpose in my life.*

His reverie was broken by the sound of Joe's voice. "Unhand my woman, boy, and give this old man a handshake."

"Handshake, nothing," laughed Luke, pulling Joe into a bear hug.

At this time, Maw and Cindy appeared from the kitchen, both smiling, arms outstretched for anyone who needed a hug. The two youngsters flew to Maw, then on to Cindy.

"Grandma Carrie, we've got a new baby calf," declared Nathan. "Papa says we might just keep it for a cow, so me and Leah, I mean Leah and I, have named her Pansy. What do you think of that name, Grandma Carrie?"

"Oh, that's just a truly special name," avowed Carrie. "With a name like that, she's certain to make a fine cow."

"Nathan and I are going to save our money and buy her a cow bell," added Leah, proud of her correct grammar. "Do you think she'll like a cow bell, Grandma Carrie?"

Giving Leah a hug, Carrie laughed, "That will be the fanciest cow in these parts, I do reckon."

Happy with the encouragement, the two ran on to play and Belinda came to give her mother and Cindy a hug.

Patting her on the shoulder as they walked toward the dining room, Carrie said, "Belinda you look so good. I'm glad to see the pink back in your cheeks and the spark back in your eyes."

"I guess I did worry everyone a bit," replied Belinda. "I've just decided to do what you always taught us, Maw ... trust God and be satisfied that He knows best. I do want a child, but if God doesn't see fit to give me one, I won't doubt his will."

Luke knew his sister. She said the right words and put a smile on her face, but he could see the pain in her eyes. *Please, God,* he whispered, *please give Belinda a child. She would make such a good mother.*

"Well," declared Cindy, "does anyone want to eat around here or do Maw and I just throw it out to the hogs?"

"I'm hungry! I'm hungry!" shouted Nathan and Leah in unison.

Winking at each other, Luke and Jessie chimed in, "I'm hungry! I'm hungry!"

With much laughter and a lightness of heart, the family gathered around the old dining room table and spent a joyous time together. After the meal Belinda whispered to Luke, "Come take a walk with me."

They stepped from the back door and walked out the little path that led to the barn. The old path was redolent with childhood memories ... walking to the hen house to get eggs and carrying them back to the house in their little baskets ... walking just past the barn to pick daisies for Maw. Such precious memories!

"There were some good times here, Luke," sighed Belinda, walking slowly, caught up in her memories. "I know there were some bad ones, especially for you, but there were good ones, too. Remember our little calf Bluebell?"

"Yeah, Sis, I remember," answered Luke, a faraway look on his face. "Yes, in many ways we had a special childhood ... except for Paw. My whole life was special ... except for Paw. He ruined everything. He hurt Maw, he put hatred in Jessie's heart at such an early age, and he took Alice from me. Paw pretty much damaged everything he touched. I wish I could let go of those memories and the pain, but I haven't been able to yet. I want to rid myself of this hate I feel, but every time I think of Alice, which is just about every waking moment, I just seem to hate him more. By the way, what do you hear from Alice?"

Belinda reached over and took Luke's arm. "I hear from her fairly often. She's trying to get on with life, but she sees it rough. I suppose you know, Luke, that she lost her little girl. I can only imagine the pain of losing a child. Then her husband was ill and she took care of him until he died. I never understood why she married Walter. He was an old man...old enough to be her father and then some. He was good to her, but she wasn't happy. Then when he died, he left her barely enough to bury him. She had to go back to work at the hotel just to pay the bills and have food to eat."

"Does she ever come back here?" asked Luke.

"No." sighed Belinda. "It's just too hard for her. There are too many memories ... of Lily and of you. She still cares for you, Brother."

"And I will always love her," said Luke, sadness in every word. "But let's change the subject. I heard what you said about not having a baby, but I also heard the truth in your voice. You can't fool your big brother, Sis. Is there no chance at all that you might have a baby?"

"Not according to Doc Moore," answered Belinda, referring to the new doctor in Haymaker. "He says it just won't happen. But, Luke, there may be another way. I haven't told anyone about this and you must promise to keep this between the two of us. Last week I was talking to Mrs. Ashton. She knows how desperately I want a child. Well, she had talked to Mr. Ashton, and they came up with an idea."

"An idea?" queried Luke. "What kind of idea?"

20

"Adoption!" squealed Belinda. "They help support the orphanage where Alice grew up and they say there are many children there who need a home. I would really like a baby, but I would take an older child. I know Joe and I could give it a good home and plenty of love. The Ashtons are going to recommend us, so that should help. Luke, I'm so excited, but I don't want to get anyone's hopes up until I know for sure, so keep my secret."

"Your secret is safe with me," declared Luke, giving her a hug, "and I'll be saying an extra prayer tonight."

With this, brother and sister walked back toward the house, arm in arm, with a little more bounce to their walk.

CHAPTER 5

An idea had been gnawing at Luke for a few days. On Monday after the chores were done and Jessie went off to work, he announced, "Maw, I think if you can spare me a while, I'll walk into Haymaker to get some things and just look around a bit."

Smiling, Carrie replied, "I think that's a splendid idea, Son, and maybe you could get me a few needed things while you're there. Now don't you hurry. You just take your time and have yourself a good day. Oh, Luke, I am so glad you are back home."

With this she wiped a tear with her apron and went back to the kitchen to finish up the bread she was making. Her heart was happier than it had been in years.

As Luke made his way to Haymaker, he was surprised to find that he had a new spring to his step and a lightness of heart that had been absent for a long time. *Lord*, he thought, *is this where you want me to be? Is there something for me here to fill this awful void? Is this where I belong?* He walked past his and Alice's house without looking in that direction and headed on to his destination. There it was! The big house where Mr. and Mrs. Ashton lived! He stood for a moment just looking and remembering all the things the Ashtons had done for him. They had taken him in when it wasn't safe to live with Paw anymore, and had treated him just like a son. They had made him feel that he had worth. It had taken awhile, for Paw had told him over and over how worthless he was and that Maw had made him a weakling. He could taste Mrs. Ashton's wonderful jelly biscuits as he walked up to the door and knocked. In seconds the door opened.

"Oh, bless my soul, if it isn't Luke Swank!" gasped Mrs. Ashton, grabbing him into her arms and squeezing until Luke was out of breath and laughing.

"I can't say as I've had a better welcome than that, except for Maw," he declared. "It is wonderful to see you, Mrs. Ashton. You're just as pretty as I remember."

He held her away from him and took in the sight. Her hair was sprinkled with gray and her skin was not quite free of lines, but the joy was still in her eyes and the softness was still in her smile. She was a beautiful lady, inside and out. "It's great to see you, Mrs. Ashton. Are you still making those tasty biscuits with that strawberry jam lathered on?"

"Why, I just took biscuits out of the oven," she laughed. "Come right on in and I'll get out the jam. Troy will be tickled pink to see you."

Following her into the house, Luke asked, "How is Mr. Ashton these days. Maw said something about trouble with his heart. Is it serious?"

Reaching up in a cabinet for strawberry jam, Mrs. Ashton replied, "Well, it's serious enough to make him give up his sheriff work. That was hard on him. He tires real easy, but all in all, he's doing well. He just has to pace himself, which he doesn't always do. I have to watch him like a hawk."

"And she is quite good at being a hawk," laughed a voice from the doorway.

Turning, Luke saw the old sheriff...the man who was more of a father to him than Tom Swank had ever been. The paleness of his face and the whiteness of his hair surprised Luke a bit. He held out his hand to Mr. Ashton, but instead of a handshake, he was pulled into a warm hug.

"How have you been, Luke boy?" he asked, tears in his eyes. "I wasn't sure you'd ever come back while I was still this side of Heaven. It's mighty good to see you, and to see how strong and good-looking you are. Must have to fight the gals off with a stick."

23

Luke laughed. "I don't have too much trouble with that, seeing as to how I don't have much use for women. I've stayed too busy to think about such stuff. It's good to see you, Sheriff."

"Now, I'm not the sheriff anymore," said Mr. Ashton, pulling out a chair at the table. "We have a new sheriff now. Sheriff Swank, I believe his name is ... and a mighty fine sheriff, I might add."

"Just can't imagine my little brother being sheriff," said Luke, shaking his head.

Mrs. Ashton set a plate of hot biscuits, butter and a jar of strawberry jam on the table and pulled out a chair. "Alright, men, eat up. And while you're eating, Luke can tell us all about himself for the last eight years. Luke, we have missed you something terrible."

Luke and the Ashtons spent a good hour going over the years they had been apart. He knew he needed to get on to some other plans he'd had for the day, but he just couldn't bring himself to leave.

"What are you going to do with yourself now that you're home?" Mr. Ashton inquired after Luke had mentioned leaving for the third time. "Any plans?"

"I don't rightly know," answered Luke. "I've got to find some way to make a living, but I don't have a clue as to what that will be. I've saved enough money to keep me going for a good while, but it won't last forever."

Silenced prevailed for a moment, but Luke could tell that Mr. Ashton had something on his mind. At last, the old man spoke.

"Luke, I don't know if this is anything that would interest you, and I don't know your money situation, but I've been notified that Morris Burke, the owner of Burke's Mercantile, plans to sell the store. It seems he and his wife are going to move out west for health reasons, and he sent me a letter asking if I would try to sell the store for him. It's something for you to think about."

"Wow!" gasped Luke. "I surely might be interested. Do you know how much he's asking?"

Mr. Ashton quoted the asking price and Luke nodded. "Let me ponder it a day or two. Can you keep it quiet that long?"

"Sure I can," declared Mr. Ashton. "I don't think Burke is in a big hurry. The store has always been a good business, and I think it would be a good investment for you. There's a young girl that runs the store right now, Luke. If you buy it, I'd ask that you give some thought to keeping her on. She needs the work and she has a business head for that sort of thing ... not to mention she has a way with people."

"She's also mighty pretty," chimed in Mrs. Ashton, turning from her cooking. "Mighty pretty."

"I'll have to agree with you, Ma'am," said Luke, smiling. "I met her the day I came back to town, and yes, she does have a way with people. She gave me a licorice stick for the sake of my old memories. I also noticed that her eyes lit up at the mention of my little brother's name."

Mr. and Mrs. Ashton shared a look. "I think she's quite taken with Jessie," said Mr. Ashton, "but I don't know that Jessie will ever give her a chance. I think he likes her a lot, but that boy is afraid to give his heart to anyone. He's full of scars that you can't see, and those are the worst kind of scars."

Luke finally took his leave with many things to ponder. He walked toward the hotel, wanting to see Belinda, but dreading the memories he would have to face. *Gotta face them some time, old boy,* he told himself. *If you're going to live here you just have to deal with the past and go on. Alice is not here anymore. She will never be a part of your life. Now deal with it!*

Straightening his shoulders, Luke climbed the wide steps to the hotel entrance. He loved the old hotel, with its tall, white pillars at the entrance. It just had the look of dignity about it. The door squeaked its years of service as he pushed it open. Looking about, he saw no one. With a mischievous gleam in his eye, he walked to the desk and rang the bell. Expecting to see Belinda, he was taken aback by the young woman who appeared from the little office behind the desk.

"May I help you, sir?" she asked, a smile of radiance on her face. She had long dark hair, large brown eyes, and looked to be in her early twenties.

"Yes, ma'am," answered Luke. "You can tell me how such a lovely lady came to work in the Haymaker Hotel. The last time I was here, that elderly woman worked here. Belinda, I believe her name was."

She stood for a moment, as though trying to decide just what to say. A giggle from the office drew her from her thoughts.

"Syrena, is this terrible man bothering you?" Belinda asked, walking toward the desk. "If so, I can call the sheriff and have him physically removed."

"N-no, Belinda," Syrena stuttered. "He's not bothering me." The crinkles on her forehead contradicted her words.

At this time, Belinda and Luke broke out in laughter as Syrena looked from one to the other.

"I'm sorry, Syrena," laughed Belinda. "I'm afraid we are having a bit of fun at your expense. This is my brother I've told you so much about. Luke, meet Syrena Blackburn, my assistant. Syrena, meet my brother Luke, the troublemaker."

Quickly regaining her composure, Syrena reached her hand to Luke. "I've heard so much about you, Luke, and it is, indeed, a pleasure to meet you."

"And it is a pleasure to meet you, Syrena," said Luke, bowing slightly. "Forgive me for being a hooligan. I just couldn't help myself."

Taking Luke by the arm, Belinda smiled warmly. "Luke, you are just what we need to take our gloom from this day. We have had some bad news this morning and neither of us knows quite what to do about it."

"Bad news?" asked Luke, a questioning look on his face. "What has happened, Sister?"

"We just found out Mrs. Faller is selling the hotel," Belinda replied. "Mr. Faller is not doing well. You know he had a stroke sometime back, and he just seems to keep fading. Mrs. Faller says the bills are piling up and she just needs to sell. She offered to let me buy it at a reasonable price, but Joe and I just don't have that much money ... nor do we want to go that far in debt. I don't know what I'll do without the hotel, though. Even if we have a child, I still plan to keep my job here."

Syrena patted Belinda's arm, a look of sadness on her face.

"Have you talked to Joe about this, Sis?" asked Luke.

She sadly shook her head. "No. But I know what he will say. We can't afford it. And he's right. Oh, Luke, it's just become such a part of me."

Luke sat silently for a moment, deep in thought. Both women were so bereft.

Finally, he said, "Sis, do you think you and Joe could afford to go in with a partner and buy the hotel?"

Wiping a tear from her eye, she answered, "Luke, I don't know of anyone who could afford it or would be interested, and I don't want to be partners with a complete stranger."

26

"I would love to go in with her and buy it," sighed Syrena, "but I don't have any money. I barely get by."

"Well, what about going in with your big brother and buying the place?" asked Luke, a smile on his face. "I've saved some money over the years. Didn't have much to spend it on. What do you think Joe would say to that?"

"Oh, Luke," she laughed, squeezing his arm tightly. "I don't know what he would say, but it's the most hope we've had. Are you sure you would want to do that?"

"I have to make a living some way if I'm going to stay here," said Luke. "The hotel always did a good business. I hope that's still true."

"It does," declared Syrena. "Business has been great this past year."

"Then tonight we will sit down and talk with Joe," said Luke. "We will just see what we can work out."

"Then come for supper tonight, Big Brother," said Belinda. "Oh, I forgot about the house. Will it be too hard for you?"

"I've got to face the memories sometime," sighed Luke. "Might as well start tonight. Just say what time and I'll be there."

Clutching her hands to her chest, she gave a nervous laugh. "How about six o'clock? And Syrena should be there, too. This decision affects her, and she loves this hotel almost as much as I do."

Luke took his leave, promising to see them both for supper. He had a great deal to think about, but in his mind he kept seeing Syrena, with the dark hair and vibrant laugh.

"No, no, boy," he declared aloud. "You will not entertain any such thoughts. You will steer clear of women."

But the thoughts still came as he made his way home.

CHAPTER 6

Luke decided not to tell his mother and Jessie about his new opportunities. It was best to know his own mind first. He simply told Maw that he was having supper with Belinda and Joe, and she was thrilled that he was getting out. His heart unusually light, he walked toward the little town of Haymaker, thinking of the decisions that lay before him. Luke had been so used to dwelling on the past it seemed odd to be contemplating a future. As he neared the little house, however, his footsteps slowed and memories came rushing in. He reached the white picket fence, but could go no further as voices from the past began screaming through his head.

You can't marry Alice! She's your sister! She's your sister ... your sister ... your sister.

"Luke, are you alright? Luke?"

The voice jarred Luke from his tormented thoughts, and as he turned, Syrena stood beside him, her hand on his arm and a worried look on her face. Yet he could not reply.

"Luke, you are so pale, and you're gripping that gate so hard your knuckles are white. Are you ill?"

Still, he couldn't speak.

"Luke, is it Alice?"

The name seemed to bring him back to reality. "How do you know about Alice?" he asked.

"Belinda told me. She wasn't being a gossip; she just told me one day when she was missing you so much. I'm sorry about it all, Luke. I can't imagine the pain you have gone through. I wish I could help."

Luke looked back at the house. "I guess this is one thing no one can help me with. It just takes time ... or at least, that's what everyone keeps telling me. I have been doing better, but the sight of the house brings everything back."

"Do you want me to go in and tell Belinda you won't be able to come to supper?" Syrena asked. "She will understand."

He stood for a moment as if considering the choice. Then he straightened his shoulders and took a deep breath. "No. No. I won't ruin Belinda's supper, and we have much to talk about. Thank you, Syrena. You came along just in time. Would you accompany me to supper, madam?"

With this he offered her his arm and they walked up the little pathway to the house. He was careful not to look toward the snowball bush.

They were all able to laugh and talk through supper. If Belinda suspected his mixed feelings, she gave no indication. Actually, she seemed extra vibrant ... not at all the depressed young woman Maw had told him about. Maybe the prospects of owning the hotel had brightened her outlook. They finished supper and gathered in the living room.

"Belinda, have you had time to talk to Joe about our discussion earlier today?" Luke asked.

Before Belinda could answer, Joe spoke. "Yes, she has, Luke. In fact, that's all she has talked about. Tell me what you see as the future for the hotel if we go with your proposal."

Luke remained quiet for a moment, and then spoke. "I really see things continuing on just as they are, Joe. I would be a silent partner. Belinda has run the hotel successfully thus far, so I don't see any need for change or any need for my input. I know nothing about running a hotel. I would be happy for us to go in fifty-fifty with the money, but the hotel will be run Belinda's way. If, later on, she should want to buy my part, I would seriously consider it."

"Oh, Luke, that sounds wonderful," sighed Belinda. "I love running the hotel, and as I said, if we should one day have a child, I could still run the hotel and be a mother."

"And I would be glad to help you with both," declared Syrena.

"That brings me to another thought," said Luke. "I know Syrena has no money now, but what about in the future when she saves some money? What would you think about letting her come in on the ownership?"

Clapping her hands, Belinda laughed, "That's exactly what Joe and I were discussing earlier. What do you think, Syrena?"

They all turned to Syrena, but she could not answer. Tears ran unchecked down her flushed cheeks.

"Well...?" said Luke.

"Well...?" said Belinda.

"Yes, oh yes!" cried Syrena. "I would love that! I would be a part of the business, and maybe even a little bitty part of a family."

"Then it is all agreed," declared Luke. "I'll go talk to Troy Ashton tomorrow morning and get his advice on how to pursue this. I have something else to talk to him about anyway."

Luke walked up the hill toward his childhood home, deep in thought. Upon reaching the porch, he sat down in Maw's rocking chair. It was such a peaceful night, and he laid his head back and listened as a cacophony of music from the crickets and bullfrogs filled the air.

Is this where I'm supposed to be, Lord? It seems so right. Am I supposed to invest in these things and stay here? Is this where I belong? Can I live here and be happy without being plagued by the memories? Please tell me, Lord.

The next thing he knew, Maw was shaking him.

"Luke, it's two in the morning," said Maw. "You must have fallen asleep and forgot to come to bed. Are you okay?"

Rubbing his eyes and yawning, Luke laughed. "I guess it was just so peaceful out here those crickets just lulled me to sleep. Yes, Maw, I'm fine. In fact, I'm the best I've been in a long, long time. I sure do love you, Maw!"

With this, he stood and gave his mother a big kiss. "Goodnight, Maw."

Carrie stood shaking her head and smiling as he walked on into the house. "Goodnight, my darling boy ... and welcome home."

The next morning Luke arose earlier than usual and had the cows milked, the hogs slopped, the chickens fed and the eggs gathered before breakfast. Carrie watched out the window as he walked toward the house whistling. In her mind she saw a little boy from years ago, carrying a basket of eggs and holding his sister's hand as she, too, carried her Easter basket with eggs. Tears rimmed her eyes, but they were tears of reminiscent joy.

"Well, Brother, looks like you got up before the rooster this morning," said Jessie, buttering one of Maw's biscuits. "Got big plans, or just trying to win 'Son of the Year' award?"

"Why, Jessie boy," Luke laughed, "I am already 'Son of the Year.' Didn't you know that?"

Shaking his head, Jessie declared. "No way. I'm the favorite around here ... and the best looking ... and the smartest. Just tell him, Maw!"

Carrie laughed, smacking him on the head gently. "I have three favorite sons, and don't either of you forget it."

"She just doesn't want to admit that I'm her favorite," whispered Jessie, nudging Luke's elbow.

"Yeah. Yeah. I hear you," laughed Luke.

"What's on your schedule for today?" asked Jessie, changing the subject.

"Well, I need to go to town if I'm not needed here. I have a few things to attend to."

"Sounds like a woman is in the picture," said Jessie. "No, now, don't try to deny it. I know the symptoms."

"Actually, it does have to do with a woman," said Luke. "As a matter of fact, it has to do with three women."

Jessie sat up straighter in his chair. "Tell me about it."

"Ask me no questions, and I'll tell you no lies," answered Luke, eyebrows raised. "Gotta get going. See you, Jess."

With that he took his leave while Jessie sat there, eyebrows drawn together in curiosity.

Mr. Ashton was sitting in his chair drinking hot tea as Mrs. Ashton showed Luke into the living room. His skin was pale, but his eyes were bright as he welcomed Luke.

"Luke, my boy!" he declared. "It's always a good day when you pay a visit. What's on your mind?"

31

Luke proceeded to tell him about the prospect of buying the hotel, along with thoughts of buying the mercantile. They talked for almost an hour and Luke could see that he was tiring his old friend.

"I'll take my leave now," he said. "I think everything is settled in my mind. I'm going to buy the mercantile and go in with Joe and Belinda on the hotel. Will you talk to your lawyer about drawing up the papers? As soon as you have rested, that is."

"I surely will," answered Mr. Ashton, with a smile. "And, Luke ... the other matter we talked about ... I'll see what I can do."

Luke shook his hand and bid him good day, heading for the mercantile.

As he came in sight of the mercantile, he could see Mandy sweeping the steps and walkway.

"Good morning, Luke!" she called. "Come by for another licorice stick?"

"I certainly did!" he laughed, holding the door for her to go inside.

Putting her broom away, she wiped her hands, then handed him a licorice stick.

As Luke enjoyed the treat, he looked at her. "I also came by for another reason."

"Oh," she said, eyebrows raised. "And what might that be?"

"I came by to tell you that there is a buyer for the mercantile."

Mandy dropped the jar she was cleaning, luckily without breaking it. Her eyes gave away the sadness and fear brought by the news.

"Do you know who is buying it?" she asked, almost in a whisper.

"Well, I hear he's a nice sort of guy," answered Luke, a twinkle in his eye.

"How soon will he take over?" she asked. "Or do you know?"

"As soon as the papers are drawn up," Luke replied. Then he added, "I also hear he is looking for a pleasant young woman to run the mercantile for him. Do you know a pleasant young woman who might be interested, Mandy?"

Hope filled her eyes. "Do you think the new owner might keep me on?"

Luke laughed. "I think he might if you keep supplying him with licorice sticks."

"You, Luke? You're the new owner?"

"I will be in a few days," he answered, smiling. "I would be very happy if you would stay on, Mandy, and run the store. I will work here some ... especially with heavier work and on days when supplies come in, but I would like for you to continue on just the way you have been running things. What do you say? Would a small raise help you to agree?"

"Oh, Luke, yes I'll stay," she laughed, clasping her hands in joy. "But I heard that part about the raise ... and I'll accept that, too."

From the mercantile, Luke continued on to the hotel to deliver more good news. He caught himself smiling.

Lord, will this work? Do I finally have a place to find peace?

CHAPTER 7

'

On Friday night Luke sat on the porch with Maw, Jessie and Cindy. It was a nice, warm night for mid-August, and Luke had been home three months. The moon shone brightly as the crickets hummed their songs. Everything seemed peaceful, and he had that "just right" feeling that permeated clear to his soul. He cleared his throat to speak.

"I have some news for all of you. I've been waiting until everything was settled before telling you my plans."

Carrie's face blanched. "Oh, Luke, tell me you're not leaving. You promised you would stay."

He reached over to pat her hand. "No, Maw. I'm not leaving. Just the opposite. I've put down permanent roots. The papers were signed today, and I'm going in with Joe and Belinda to buy the Haymaker Hotel."

"What?" cried Cindy. "I knew the hotel was for sale. Belinda has mourned over it something terrible for the past several days. You bought it, Luke? You and Belinda and Joe are partners? I will still have a place to work?"

"Yes, to all of those questions," laughed Luke. "The hotel will be run the same as it has been. I will be a silent partner."

"I must say, Brother, this is a shock ... although a very pleasant one," said Jessie. "I didn't know I had a rich brother. Now I'll be cared for in my old age."

"Luke, that is such blessed news," said Carrie. "Now I know you are home to stay where you belong, and I'm so happy for Belinda. She's had so many disappointments lately, and the loss of the hotel would have been more than she could bear. But what about Syrena? Will she be able to stay on?"

"Just as before," nodded Luke. "She has even been given the option of buying into the partnership when she has the money."

All four sat in silence, absorbing the good news.

"There's more," said Luke. "I've also bought Berke's Mercantile."

"Whhaatt?" they all exclaimed.

"Mr. Ashton told me several days ago that Morris Berke was going to sell and move out west for his health. He asked if I would be interested. After a few days of pondering, I decided to buy it."

"What about Mandy?" asked Jessie, his forehead crinkling with concern. "She really needs a job, Luke."

Luke smiled. "That's already taken care of. Mandy will continue to run the store with my help from time to time. I've even given her a raise. She's a capable and pleasant young woman, and she gets a twinkle in her eye every time my little brother's name is mentioned."

Jessie chose to ignore the comment, but his beet-red face gave away his feelings.

"Will you still call it Berke's Mercantile?" asked Cindy. "That seems unfitting now that Mr. Berke doesn't own it. I think you should call it Luke's Mercantile."

"I second that," injected Carrie.

"I third that," added Jessie.

"Then I guess it will be Luke's Mercantile," said Luke. "I kind of like the sound of that."

In the ensuing weeks Luke put in much needed hours on the farm. Jessie helped when he could, but his job as sheriff demanded most of his time. They had built new fences and repaired old ones, cut and stacked hay, patched up the pig sty and were in the process of building Maw a brand new chicken coop. Next week they planned to paint the little picket fence around the yard.

It was a sunny Friday afternoon and as the two brothers worked they talked.

"Do you think Clay is ever coming back home?" Luke asked Jessie. "It's been a long while from what Maw tells me."

Jessie paused to wipe the sweat from his forehead with his sleeve. "I wish he would. Maw misses him much more than she will let on. I don't know what the holdup is with him. I know he loves the horse training and all, but it's got to be something else. I wonder if Abigail might have something to do with it. Maybe she doesn't want Clay to come back here."

"Why would that be?" asked Luke.

"I don't know," answered Jessie. "It's just a hunch, I guess. We'd better be finishing up here, Luke. Uncle Nate will be over pretty soon and we'll need to eat and clear out."

Luke turned a puzzled face to Jessie. "Uncle Nate? I didn't know he was coming to supper. And what does that have to do with eating and clearing out?"

"Oh, you didn't know," laughed Jessie, giving Luke that 'I know something you don't know' look.

"Okay, Brother. Out with it!"

"You didn't know that Uncle Nate's been coming a-courting?" asked Jessie, a mixture of mischief and laughter in his eyes.

The look on Luke's face was worth it all. "Coming a-courting? Who's he courting?"

Then it hit him without Jessie saying a word.

"Uncle Nate and Maw? Uncle Nate's coming to see Maw?"

"That would be correct," replied Jessie, nodding his head to emphasize his answer. "Aunt Charlotte died about two years ago from a heart problem. Then about a year ago he started dropping by every now and then ... and then he suddenly started coming for Saturday evening supper, after which he and Maw would sit on the porch and talk."

Luke sat for a minute trying to absorb this latest bit of news. *Maw and Uncle Nate?*

"Is it serious?" he asked.

"Oh, it is with Nate," Jessie replied. "You can see it in his eyes every time he looks at Maw. Now with Maw ... I don't think so. I think she could love Nate if she would let herself, but after what she went through with Paw, I don't know that Maw could ever allow herself to love another man. To tell you the truth, Luke, I wish she would fall in love with him. Nate's a good man...nothing like Paw. He loved Charlotte deeply and was always good to her. The last months of her life he took care of her twenty-four hours a day. Whether this will amount to anything someday, I don't have a clue, but in the meantime, it's good companionship for Maw."

"Well, I'll be!" said Luke, almost in a whisper. Seems like there were certain things Maw had left out of her letters.

They finished up their work and went inside to wash up. Sure as shooting, at five o'clock Uncle Nate came up the front steps and knocked lightly on the door. Luke could have gotten to the door more quickly, but he waited to see what Maw would do. She turned from the stove, wiped her hands on her apron, smoothed back some straying wisps of hair and went to answer the door.

"Why, Nate, how good to see you," she said. "Supper's almost ready. I made chicken and dumplings and your favorite ... peach pie."

Nate looked at Carrie and Luke could see exactly what Jessie had talked about. This man was absolutely in love with Maw. His eyes were filled not only with love, but also admiration and respect. That look won Luke over. This man would be good for Maw.

"My stomach's been crying out all week for your peach pie, Carrie," Nate said, rubbing his middle. "How did you know?"

"I always knew you liked peach pie, Nate. You tell me all the time." With this Carrie laughed in a way Luke hadn't heard her laugh in years.

"Nate," she continued, "you haven't seen Luke since he came home."

Reaching out his hand, Luke greeted him, "Hi, Uncle Nate. It's good to see you. It's been a long time. Sorry to hear about Aunt Charlotte."

Nate shook his hand vigorously. "Thanks, Luke. You're sure looking good, and I know you've brought joy to your mother by coming home. Hope you've come back to stay."

"That I have, Nate," he answered. "That I have."

Cindy and Jessie arrived within minutes and they all sat down for supper. The talk around the table was jovial and easy. Luke sat back and

37

just looked for a moment, taking it all in. *This is what our family could have been like,* he thought, *if only Paw had been like Nate. If only Paw's family had been enough for him.*

After supper, Cindy and Luke volunteered to do the dishes and Jessie went to his room to catch up on paperwork. Maw and Nate retired to the front porch.

CHAPTER 8

Nate continued to come calling every Saturday after that, and whether she would admit it or not, Maw looked forward to it. She would "spiff up" just a little more on Saturdays and cook like she was feeding a king. Actually, Luke began to look forward to it, too. He liked Nate and liked to talk to him. Jessie and Cindy seemed to be taken with him as well.

It was a Sunday, a few weeks after Luke had gotten reacquainted with Nate, and Maw was fixing Sunday dinner for all of her "clan," as she called them. Nate didn't attend these dinners, but Luke felt it was only a matter of time. Maw and Cindy were in the kitchen cooking and Luke was setting the table. Jessie had gone to check on the new calf born just hours before. All of a sudden Luke heard the screen door slam.

"Maw? Are you in here?"

It was Belinda's voice and Luke couldn't tell if she was scared, hurt or excited.

"Maw? Where are you?"

Carrie came hurriedly through the dining room, wiping her hands on a towel draped over her shoulder. "Belinda, what ever is the matter?"

Belinda swept through the house and drew her mother into a crushing embrace.

"Oh, Maw," she exclaimed, "I'm going to have a baby!"

"A baby!" gasped Maw. "You're going to have a baby? You're with child?"

"Well, not exactly," responded Belinda, relaxing her hold on Maw.

"Not exactly!" laughed Cindy, coming next to them. "Belinda, either you are pregnant or you're not ... and either you're going to have a baby or you're not. Which is it?"

Belinda dropped into a chair, spent from the excitement.

"Joe, you tell them," she said. "Oh, no, don't. I have to tell this myself."

Carrie sat down next to Belinda and took her hand. "Honey, just calm yourself and tell us your news. Are you with child?"

"No. No, I'm not pregnant," answered Belinda. "But I'm going to have a baby."

They all just looked at each other in confusion.

Able to stand the confusion no longer, Joe said. "She's not going to have a baby, but we're going to get a baby. Now, Belinda, tell them your news."

She drew a deep breath as though she needed fortification. "We received a call from the orphanage where Alice grew up. About two weeks ago they received a baby whose mother had died a few days after it was born due to complications from giving birth. The mother herself had once been an orphan. She was married, so the father took the child to raise alone. When the baby was three months old, the father, also an orphan, was killed in a logging accident. There was no one to take the baby ... a little girl ... so she was given to the orphanage. Mr. and Mrs. Ashton had recommended Joe and me as candidates for adoption. The baby is now four months old and they say we can come and get her next week. Some papers have to be filled out, but that's all there is to it. Since there is no family, everything will go quickly. I'm going to be a mother! Isn't that just the grandest news in the world, Maw?"

"I reckon it surely is, honey," laughed Maw, tears flowing freely down her cheeks. "I don't know of any better news we could have heard."

"And I'm just so happy for you," said Cindy, hugging her big sister.

"Add me to that list," said Luke, hugging her tightly.

"And me," added Jessie, who had come into the house in time to hear it all.

"Just wait until Ady Rose hears this," laughed Cindy. "She'll squeal 'til the roof comes off."

About that time Ady Rose and Willy arrived with their two children, and Belinda reiterated the entire story, a little more calmly this time. As they sat around the table enjoying Maw's good meal, there were dozens of questions.

"Do you have any baby clothes or furniture?" asked Cindy, always the practical one.

"I don't have anything," answered Belinda. "Tomorrow we're going to get the things we absolutely need. Then we'll get more as we can. This has happened so suddenly."

"We have a baby crib you can use, Sis," said Ady Rose. "You may want to get one of your own, but it will do until you have time to shop."

"Oh, I would love using Leah and Nathan's old crib," exclaimed Belinda. "It will make it seem even more special."

"Yeah," said Nathan, puffing out his chest. "I don't need such stuff anymore."

This brought volumes of laughter.

"When will you go get my new granddaughter?" inquired Carrie, liking the sound of the term 'granddaughter.'

"They have scheduled it for Thursday," said Joe. "It will take them a while to get the papers fixed up."

"What's this baby going to be for us?" asked Nathan, eyebrows drawn together as he tried to figure out the situation.

"She will be our cousin, Nathan," said Leah. "Don't you know anything?"

"That will be enough, young lady," admonished Willy. "Nathan was just making sure of things. Nothing wrong with that."

The menfolk went on out to the porch while the women stayed inside to clean up.

"I'm scared, Maw," confessed Belinda, when the four women were alone. "I've wanted this for so long, and now I'm scared I won't know how to be a good mother."

"It's natural to be a little afraid, my darling girl," soothed Carrie. "I felt the same way before Luke was born. I think all mothers feel that apprehension. But Belinda, you will make a wonderful mother. You were born to be a mother, just like Ady Rose was."

"I'm still afraid sometimes," laughed Ady Rose. "If you've been around those two of mine, you will understand that."

On Monday and Tuesday Joe and Belinda, with the help of family and friends, put together a nursery for their new little daughter. Maw stayed home, busy with needle and thread, making diapers and gowns. She could feel the joy going into every stitch.

"Thank you, my dear Savior," she whispered. "You have taken days of pain and trial and replaced with them with love and joy. Only you could do that. Thank you, Lord. Help Belinda and Joe in this new stage of their life, and bless this little child. May it always know love."

The big day finally arrived. It was agreed that the family would wait until Friday, the day after they went to pick up the baby, and then all would gather at Joe's and Belinda's to welcome her. Maw was as excited as the day she first gave birth. They arrived at six o'clock, laden with food so Belinda wouldn't have to cook. As the food was placed on the table, Belinda walked into the room carrying a precious bundle that was wrapped in pink. Joe walked behind her, every bit the proud father.

"Maw," said Belinda quietly, "meet your new granddaughter."

Carrie reached for her, and Belinda placed her in her arms. Carrie looked at her in wonder.

"Why, she reminds me of Cindy when she was born," gasped Carrie. "Look at her, Ady Rose. Do you see the resemblance?"

"Well, I'll be," laughed Ady Rose. "She does look a lot like her. See, this baby was just meant for this family. What have you named her, Belinda?"

"We haven't named her," answered Belinda. "She already had a name given to her by her birth parents, so we decided she should keep that name. Besides, it's a very special name."

"Oh?" said Luke. "What is this special name?"

"You won't believe this," answered Belinda, eyes gleaming. "Her name is Carrie ... Carrie Mae."

There was an audible gasp throughout the room.

"See, I told you!" squealed Ady Rose. "She was meant for this family."

Nodding, Belinda added, "We've decided to call her Cammy, to make it short for Carrie Mae. So, everyone, meet Cammy, our new daughter."

"Welcome to our family, Cammy," whispered Carrie. "We promise you all the love you will ever need ... and then some ... for this is a family of great love."

"Belinda," said Cindy, "will you be able to take care of her and run the hotel and dress shop now that I'm back to teaching and will only be able to help part-time? I know Syrena will be there, but business is good right now. Don't you think you might need to hire some extra help?"

Belinda and Joe exchanged a look.

"Actually we have been thinking about that," said Belinda. "We have come up with an idea."

She paused, as though afraid to continue.

"Maw, what would you think about coming to work at the hotel dress shop maybe two days a week ... only for a few months. I know you have a lot to do, but it would be good if Cammy could be around family during her first months with us."

All eyes turned to Carrie. Luke was the first to speak.

"I think it would be a grand idea, Maw. You could sew part of the time and take care of your new granddaughter part of the time. You could get to know each other."

"Sounds like a good idea to me," injected Jessie.

"Oh, Maw, you would love it," exclaimed Ady Rose. "Please say yes."

There was silence for a moment.

"Yes!" laughed Carrie. "I would love to be near Cammy and cuddle her and spoil her."

"Now, let's hold off on that spoiling," said Joe, with a laugh. "I'm the one who will have to get up at night."

"Just listen to that," said Willy. "I'll bet I know who will do most of the spoiling of that little girl. Her daddy, that's who!"

"There's one more thing we wanted to talk to everyone about," said Belinda, her eyes filled with apprehension.

"What is it, darling?" asked Carrie. "Is something wrong?"

"Well, n-no," stammered Belinda. "At least I hope it won't be wrong. You see, we really need more help at the hotel. We need someone to help change the rooms each day and do the washing and things like that."

"So what's the problem?" asked Jessie. "Is there no one to hire?"

"There is someone," answered Belinda. "She came to me last week asking for work."

"Then what's the problem?" asked Luke.

"We're not sure Maw would approve," said Belinda.

"Just tell them, Belinda," urged Joe. "Maw will tell you if it bothers her or not, and if it does, then we won't hire her."

"Who is this you are so worried that I won't approve of?" questioned Carrie.

"It's Matildy Willis' youngest daughter, Maw," said Belinda quickly before she lost her nerve. "Her name is Nettie. She's not like the rest of them. She came and talked to me and said she really wanted to make something of her life, and I believe her. I would like to give her a try, but I don't want to bring up the past and hurt you. So just tell me how you feel, Maw."

"Belinda, hiring this girl won't hurt me," answered Carrie. "She is not to blame for her mother's way of life or that of her sisters. She is a child of God just like the rest of us. If He can forgive us for our sins, how can I judge others? I don't even harbor bad feelings toward Lizzie. No one made Tom do the things he did. Hire her, daughter. Guide her and give her a chance for a better life. If you are afraid it would be hard for me to work with her, then set your mind at rest. I will be just fine."

Belinda handed the baby to Ady Rose and ran to her mother.

"Maw, you are the very best! I love you so much."

The rest of the afternoon was spent passing Cammy around, giving advice on taking care of babies, setting up Maw's schedule for work and just having fun. Luke found himself watching the scene playing out before him and loving the family he had been away from for so long.

If only Alice could be here, he thought. *She would have loved every minute of this. We could have been holding our own children by now. If only....*

44

CHAPTER 9

Over the next few weeks everyone settled into a routine. Maw worked at the dress shop on Tuesdays and Wednesdays and loved every minute of it. Her face seemed to glow in her new-found happiness. Each afternoon when she came home, she regaled them with stories of Cammy and sometimes of people who came into the shop. Luke couldn't remember seeing her happier. He, Jessie and Cindy helped with the household chores so she could get some rest.

It was the first Friday in October and new merchandise would be arriving for the mercantile, so Luke headed into town to unload it from the train and haul it to the store. He had enlisted Jessie's help. As they pulled up in front of the store, Mandy came hurrying out the door. Luke couldn't help but notice that she had taken a little extra care with her appearance .

"Good morning, Luke ... and Jessie!" she called, her eyes on Jessie alone.

"Why, good morning," answered Luke. "I must say, you look nice today, Mandy. Don't you think so, Jessie?"

"Wh-what?" stammered Jessie, his face redder than the beets Maw canned. "Oh, yes, very nice."

"You sure know how to pay a girl a compliment, Jessie," laughed Mandy.

"Sorry, Mandy," said Jessie, straightening his shoulders. "You do, indeed, look nice today. Is that a new dress?"

"As a matter of fact, it is," answered Mandy. "Thank you for noticing. I finished it just yesterday. Let me grab an apron and I'll help you nice gentlemen carry all of this in."

She and Luke kept the conversation flowing as they unloaded the merchandise, with little input from Jessie. If his silence bothered her, she never let it show, but Luke could see that she was in love with his brother.

Why can't he see how beautiful and special she is, thought Luke. *She's just what my little brother needs. Lord, open his heart before it's too late.*

They worked for about two hours, carrying in the wares, clearing shelf space and putting some in the storage room. When it was finished, they all breathed a happy sigh.

"I need to work a little while on some of the storage shelves that are getting wobbly," said Luke. "Jessie, why don't you take Mandy over to the diner and the two of you have a bite to eat. I know you've both worked up an appetite."

He could see the paleness of Jessie's face, and his intake of breath was almost audible. Before Jessie could object, however, Mandy spoke.

"That would be delightful. I only had time for coffee and a biscuit for breakfast and my stomach is about to get acquainted with my backbone. Let's go, Jessie."

With this, she looped her arm through Jessie's and led the poor, bewildered man out the door. Luke stood in the doorway, watching and laughing inside. *Jessie, old boy,* he thought, *you don't stand a chance.*

After finishing the shelves at the back of the mercantile, Luke turned things back over to the radiantly happy Mandy, and left to go see Troy and Mabel Ashton. He wanted to see if Mr. Ashton had been able to help him with an idea he had told him about.

"Come in, Luke," invited Mrs. Ashton, in a quiet voice. Her face seemed to wear a look of worry.

"Is everything alright, Mrs. Ashton?" asked Luke. "Do I need to come back another time?"

"No, dear," she answered, motioning with her hand for him to follow her. "Troy has just had a bad night. Maybe your visit will help."

Then she stopped before going on toward the sitting room. "Luke, he is fading fast. To be honest, I don't think I have much more time with him."

Her eyes filled with tears and she quickly tried to wipe them away.

"What can I do?" asked Luke, putting his arm around her. "You know I'll do anything you ask."

She smiled and patted his arm. "You are doing it by just being here. He loves you like a son, Luke. We both do. Now come along before he gets the idea we are talking about him."

Luke was taken aback by the change in Mr. Ashton from just a few days before. Even his lips were white and all luster was gone from his eyes. Yet, still he managed a light smile as Luke entered the room. He reached out his hand and Luke took it in his, noticing the frailty. Mrs. Ashton left them to their talk.

"How are you, Mr. Ashton?" Luke asked, the concern obvious in his voice.

"Not long for this world, my boy. Not long for this world."

"Don't try to talk," said Luke. "Let me just sit here with you for awhile."

"No, there is much to say," responded Mr. Ashton. "Much to say and a short time to say it. Luke, when I am gone, my dear wife will go back north to be with her kinfolk. Will you promise to see to her until she leaves? She's a strong woman, but she will need help."

"I give you my word," answered Luke. "She's like a second mother to me."

"Luke, there's more I want to talk to you about, and it must be said. Just bear with me as I run out of breath easily."

He sat in silence for a moment as Luke waited patiently, their hands joined.

"It's about Jessie," he said finally. "That boy has something eating away inside of him, and he needs to let it go. He needs to talk to Carrie, Luke. I can't tell you what it's about, but he knows. Just see that he has that talk, Luke. He'll never be happy until he does."

Luke was puzzled but assured Mr. Ashton that he would see to the matter. They talked about Luke's reason for coming, and then Mr. Ashton

47

went over some other final details with him. Luke left with a heavy heart, wondering if he would ever see his dear friend again.

The following Saturday evening Nate came by once more and they all had supper together. Luke was warming to the idea of him and Maw right quickly. Nate was nothing like Paw, and, although Maw would never admit it, he saw a little sparkle in her eye when Nate arrived.

"Nate," said Luke, clearing his throat and pushing back from the table, "why don't you come over for Sunday dinner tomorrow. It's just family and you're a part of our family. We'd be glad to have you, wouldn't we, Maw?"

Nate looked quickly at Carrie.

"Yes, Nate," she said, "we would enjoy having you with us. Won't you come?"

The happiness showed in his eyes as he nodded. "Can't think of anything I'd rather do. Thanks, Luke ... and Carrie."

With this, Luke arose from the table, feeling quite satisfied with himself. Jessie and Cindy were fighting hard, he could tell, to hide their laughter.

"You two go sit a spell now," offered Cindy. "We'll take care of everything in here."

The next day all the siblings arrived with their families and enjoyed another Sunday dinner. Nate was there right on time. Afterword, they all adjourned to the front porch, with Leah and Nathan playing in the yard and little Cammy snoozing away in the little cradle Maw had used for all of them. After some small talk and laughter, Luke cleared his throat, which was always a sign he had something to say.

"I have something I need to talk to Cindy about," he began, "but it affects all of us, so I wanted to do it with everyone here."

"To me?" gasped Cindy. "Is something wrong, Luke?"

"On the contrary," answered Luke. "I think it's a very good thing, but I don't know how you will feel or how Maw and the rest will feel."

Reaching to pat his hand, Carrie said, "Luke, the best way is to just say what's on your mind. I know anything you have to say will be said with love."

"Well..." began Luke. "We all know how Cindy loves to teach, and she's pretty well made it clear that she has settled on that for her life's work.

I went to talk with Mr. Ashton the other day to see what information he could find about a certain matter. You see, there's a teacher's school...or I think they call it the State Teachers' School...about a day's travel by train from here. You can go there for a year and get a teaching certificate. With that, you could get a job almost anywhere and you would be paid more money."

"I've heard of it," said Cindy, sitting straighter in her chair. "I'm afraid it's above my budget, though, and I'm needed here and at the hotel."

"I will pay your tuition if you will go, Cindy," said Luke. "I think you should have the chance to fulfill your dream. Now it was too late to get you in this fall, so you won't begin until next September. That gives you plenty of time to prepare."

"I think it's a wonderful idea," injected Ady Rose. "You will make a marvelous teacher, Cindy, and you deserve it. You are always making everyone happy, so now let someone make you happy. Luke this is a wonderful, loving thing you are doing."

"I agree," said Belinda. "Cindy, you are a great help at the hotel, but you deserve to follow your dream. We will make out. Please don't let this chance pass you by."

There was silence for a moment as all eyes turned to Carrie.

"Maw?" said Cindy.

After just another moment of silence, Carrie turned to Cindy.

"I don't have to tell you that I will be lost without you, my dear. However, I would be very disappointed if you didn't take this opportunity. God has given you a gift, Cindy, and when God gives us a gift, he expects us to use it. You have my blessing, dear heart. And Luke, I can't tell you how proud I am of you."

"Well, Cindy?" said Luke.

A bright smile crept gently from her lips to her eyes.

"Yes, Luke! Oh, yes! I would love to go to the Teachers' School. Thank you!"

With this, she threw her arms around Luke, and then, in turn, hugged everyone there. Soon everyone was crying and laughing. Carrie looked on with tear-filled eyes, wondering how one could feel so much happiness and sadness at the same time.

It's only for a year, she told herself, but a voice whispered, *Then what?*

CHAPTER 10

Two weeks before Thanksgiving Troy Ashton passed away. Jessie came home from work with the news, struggling to hold back the tears.

"He was a good man," said Carrie. "There's no telling how many people he has helped through the years, but none more than this family. I shiver to think of what might have happened to you, Luke, if he hadn't removed you from this house."

"He was just like a father to me," said Luke, tears running unchecked down his face and making droplets on his shirt. "He was even more than a father ... he was my trusted friend."

"And he has been the same to me," added Jessie, wiping his own tears. "He never turned me away when I needed his help."

"This will be so hard on Mrs. Ashton," said Cindy softly. "They were a close couple ... so devoted to each other. That's how marriage is supposed to be."

They all sat in silence for awhile, each caught up in their own memories of the life Mr. Ashton had lived.

Breaking the silence, Carrie asked, "Do you have any word about the arrangements, Jessie?"

"Not yet," he replied. "I suppose we will know tomorrow. Mrs. Ashton said he made his own plans sometime back. That's just like him, trying to make it easier on everyone."

The funeral was held two days later, a sunny, warm day for mid-November. It seemed the entire town and beyond was in attendance. Brother Harold from the Primitive Baptist Church presided, and both Luke and Jessie gave a eulogy in acquiescence to Mrs. Ashton's request. They each talked about the example Mr. Ashton set for others.

"He was a man who gave, not only of his assets," said Luke, "he gave of himself and he gave from the heart. He was like a father to me, and he encouraged me at a time when I was down on myself and my life seemed hopeless. I hope I can be at least half the man he was. I'm sure going to miss him."

Jessie talked about replacing Mr. Ashton as sheriff.

"I was scared to death," he admitted, "but Mr. Ashton trained me and advised me. He gave me courage when I had none. This community has lost a great man."

After the burial, Mrs. Ashton took both of them aside. "Boys, I would like you to come by the house tomorrow at eleven. Troy's lawyer, Sam Lundy, will be there to read the will. Can you come?"

Luke and Jessie exchanged perplexed looks and then nodded. "We'll be there," said Luke.

"Thank you," she said, wiping her tears. "I plan to leave for New York in two weeks and I want everything taken care of before then. I hate to leave and yet I can't stay without Troy. I have two sisters and nieces and nephews there, and they have asked me to come live with them."

The next day both boys arrived precisely at eleven. No one else was there besides Mrs. Ashton and Mr. Lundy.

"We will get right to this," said an unsmiling Mr. Lundy.

As he read the will, Luke and Jessie sat silently, wondering why they needed to be there. Then all of a sudden, Luke heard his name.

"To Luke Thomas Swank, I leave the sum of fifty thousand dollars to be used as he sees fit. To Jessie Silas Swank, I leave my house and the twenty acres surrounding it. To Tiny Alice Warren, I leave the sum of fifty thousand dollars to be used as she sees fit. These are the three children Mrs. Ashton and I love as our own, and we are thankful we could share their lives. I have no doubt they will use the money wisely and with much prayer."

When the reading was concluded, Luke and Jessie sat in stunned silence. Finally, Mrs. Ashton spoke.

"You must accept this inheritance because of the love my husband and I have for you. You brought more joy to our lives than you could ever know. I have plenty to live on for the rest of my life, and this is what Troy wanted and what I want."

Kneeling in front of her, Luke took her hand. "I don't know what to say, Mrs. Ashton. You have both given so much to me, but most importantly, you gave your love. Thank you for that."

Jessie joined Luke. "You were there for us and for Maw when our lives were a mess. I will never forget that."

Suddenly Luke rose. "What about Alice? Does she know about this?"

"I asked her to come for the reading," said Mrs. Ashton, "but she thought it might be too difficult for everyone. Mr. Lundy will get in touch with her tomorrow and will see that she gets the money."

Luke and Jessie left a short time later, assuring Mrs. Ashton they would be there in the days ahead to help her wrap up things and get ready for her departure. It was a sad and confusing time, and the boys said little on their way home.

Finally Jessie spoke. "I can't believe Mr. Ashton left us something. Luke, I don't even know what to do with a house and land."

"And I don't know what to do with fifty thousand dollars," laughed Luke nervously. "I tell you what, Jessie, let's use it for some good. If we ask God, I know he will show us just what to use it for."

"God and I don't talk much anymore, Brother," answered Jessie. "Maybe you better ask Him."

Luke pondered the answer for a moment and then spoke. "Jessie, Mr. Ashton spoke to me about you a few days before he died. I don't know exactly what he meant, but he said you needed to talk to Maw about something, and that you wouldn't find peace until you do."

Jessie looked away, making no response.

"Jessie?" said Luke. "Did you hear me? Do you know what he's talking about?"

"Yes, I know," answered Jessie. "And I know he's right, but I just can't tell you about it, Luke. Maw is the one I need to talk to. I just don't know how to go about it."

"Then let's pray, Jessie," said Luke, taking him by the shoulder. "Let's pray right now. That's what Maw and Grandpa Silas always did, and if they did it, it must be the right way."

They stopped by the side of the road, Luke with his hand still on Jessie's shoulder.

"God," he began, "I don't know much lately about talking to you, but we sure need your help. Whatever Jessie is carrying around, would you just help him get it off his chest? I want him to be happy, God, and I want him to have a good life. So if you could just see your way clear, help him in this. And while you're at it, God, would you please help us to use this inheritance from Mr. Ashton to do some good. Thank you for sending him and Mrs. Ashton into our lives, and just help us to help someone the way they helped us. I do thank you, God. Amen."

After a few seconds, Jessie looked up with a smile. "I don't know why exactly, Luke, but I sorta feel peaceful."

They walked on home in silence, feeling a new peace and wondering what God had in store for them. That night they told Carrie about their inheritance and how they wanted to use it for some good.

"Just don't get in a hurry," said Carrie. "Listen, watch and God will show you. It may be a week from now or it may be a year from now. Just be patient and believe."

"I'm glad they left something for Alice," said Luke. "I know she can use the money, and she loved the two of them. She deserves a break in life."

"She certainly does," declared Carrie.

Ten days later they said goodbye to Mrs. Ashton as she left for New York, promising to write often. The next day was Thanksgiving and, as usual, they gathered with Maw as a family, Nate included. Also joining them were Mandy and Syrena who had no family to be with. It was also due to some sneaky planning by Belinda and Ady Rose. As they gathered around an abundant table, Nate was asked to lead the blessing of the food.

"Heavenly Father," he began, "we do thank you for all this good food before us and for the loving hands that fixed it. Thank you that we can all be together ... and God, I thank you that this family took a lonely old man like me and made me a part of such a good loving family. They have given me more joy than they know. We thank you for our loved ones who have gone on to be with you, 'cause we still have our memories of them. We thank you for your love and mercy. Amen."

Eyes were damp as they raised their heads.

I can't ever remember Tom praying, thought Carrie as she looked at Nate.

Then they ate and laughed and talked just like families are supposed to do.

Just as Maw and Cindy were handing out desserts, there was a light knock at the front door.

"I'll get it," said Luke. "Maybe it's a hungry soul to eat some of this food that's left over."

He walked to the door and opened it. Then his heart began beating the sound of a thousand drums. He could not speak ... he could barely breathe ... for there, on the front porch stood Alice. She had aged a little and looked tired, but Luke thought she was the most magnificent sight he had ever seen.

"Hello, Luke," she said, smiling, with a mixture of joy and sadness in her eyes. "It's been a long time."

Luke could say nothing.

"Luke, who is it?" called Carrie. "Invite them in for some food. We have plenty."

Luke could still say nothing.

"Luke, who...." asked Carrie, then stopping as she saw who stood at the door.

"Hello, Aunt Carrie," said Alice. "I guess I've surprised everyone."

"Oh, my darling girl!" cried Carrie. "I am surprised but delighted. It is so good to see you! Luke, open the door, child."

Finally clearing his head enough to obey, Luke opened the door, still unable to speak. He could not swallow and his lips refused to move. By this time Belinda and Ady Rose were halfway through the living room squealing loud enough for the neighbors to hear.

"Alice!" they squealed. "Oh, this is truly a wonderful Thanksgiving!"

The rest of the family joined in welcoming her, insisting that she sit down and eat. Cindy arranged a chair right next to Luke, who remained in a daze. He could do nothing but look at Alice. After the meal was finished, they adjourned to enjoy the unusual fall warmth of the front porch, allowing Leah and Nathan a chance to run off some energy in the yard. Nate, Willy and Joe joined the children in a game of catch, so that Carrie and her family could have Alice to themselves.

"We are so glad you could spend Thanksgiving with us, Alice?"said Belinda. "It's been a long time and I was afraid I would never see you again. Is there something special that brings you back?"

"Well, yes," replied Alice. "There are several things, but I will start at the beginning. You see, I made a vow many, many years ago that I would find all of my siblings. It broke my heart when Lily sent us away, but it tore my heart to shreds when we were separated. I made that vow the very day Belle and Homer were adopted and James and I were left at the orphanage. They wouldn't even let us see them to say goodbye. Then I lost James ... dear, sweet James. But I never stopped searching ... and now it has paid off ... well, in a manner of speaking."

A tear trickled down her wan cheek as she uttered the last words.

"What do you mean by that?" asked Ady Rose, almost in a whisper, as though she feared the answer.

"I found Homer," said Alice. He is living in Ohio and is the pastor of a church up there."

"A pastor?" said Carrie. "A pastor. Why that is just the best thing I've ever heard. That means he has found peace. Is he married? Does he have children?"

"Yes and yes," answered Alice with a light laugh. "He is married. Her name is Trula and they have five children ... little stair steps he told me. Four boys and one girl. I haven't seen him or met his family yet, but they are coming soon for a visit. I can't tell you how much I want to see my little brother again."

"And what about Belle?" asked Belinda.

Alice paused, trying to find the courage to answer. She sadly shook her head. "Belle is dead, I'm afraid."

"Oh, no," gasped Cindy. "She would be so young. Do you know what caused her death?"

"Yes," answered Alice. "Her death was due to childbirth."

"She had a baby?" said Carrie. "Oh, how sad. Where is the baby? Did it live?"

"I don't know," answered Alice. "I mean, yes, it lived, but I don't know where it is. I've been trying to find out. I know that she was married and her husband kept the child after her death, but then he died in an accident. Neither of them had any family, so the baby was put in an orphanage, but I can't find out any more than that. I've contacted several orphanages, but they either haven't heard of Belle, or refuse to give out information. I want to know more. I must find out if it is well cared for. I know how orphanages can be."

There was utter silence as they all looked from one to the other. Belinda was ghostly white.

"Did you check at the orphanage where you lived?" asked Ady Rose, looking from Belinda, to Carrie, and then to Alice.

"I did," nodded Alice, "but they said they were not allowed to tell me anything."

"Alice, how old would the baby be?" Belinda asked, her voice quivering.

"I'm not quite sure," Alice replied. "Less than a year. I am told they named her, and you would never believe the name."

"Carrie!" they all answered together.

Alice looked around at all the smiling faces bewildered. "Why, how did you know? Have you been searching, too?"

With this, Belinda arose, went over to the cradle, and picked up Cammy.

"From all you have told us, Alice, I believe without a doubt, mine and Joe's newly adopted daughter may just be Belle's birth child. Meet Carrie Mae. We call her Cammy."

Belinda placed the baby in Alice's arms, and Alice held the child to her breast, unable to speak.

"That explains so much!" exclaimed Cindy. "That's why she was named Carrie, and remember when you first saw her, Maw? You said she looked just like me as a baby. It has to be the same baby!"

By this time, having heard the excitement on the porch, the men had rejoined them.

"Let me ask you this, Alice," said Joe. "You said the father was killed in an accident. Do you know what kind of accident?"

Alice nodded. "Yes, it was a logging accident. Some logs broke loose and rolled over him. I've been told he was a good man and he and Belle were very much in love. It is such a blessing to know that Belle had some love in her life."

Again, they all looked at each other.

"There's no doubt," said Belinda. "I knew Cammy was special right from the start. Now we all know just how special she really is."

"And," added Ady Rose, "one reason you may have had a hard time finding her is because the name Belle used was *Arabella*. Apparently, her adoptive parents had renamed her.

Alice sat beaming down at the little girl. "My little niece," she said. "Hi, Cammy. I'm your Aunt Alice."

"God moves in mysterious ways," said Carrie, her heart so full that she felt it would burst. "Out of so much bad in our lives, He still fills it with good."

About that time, Cammy let out a loud wail, and this brought laughter from everyone.

"I guess this little "good" in our lives thinks it's time to be fed," laughed Belinda.

As Belinda left to feed her, the others sat talking about life and its surprises, and how God is always in control. They had lost Belle, but God had sent Cammy to them.

Belle must be looking down and rejoicing, thought Carrie.

CHAPTER 11

There was much to talk about as Alice sat feeding and rocking Cammy. Luke looked on, enjoying the sight and the joy in Alice's eyes.

This is what it would have been like, he thought, *if we could have married and had our own children. I could have seen this joy in her eyes every single day. If only....*

Suddenly Luke jumped up from his chair and left the room. The sight was more than he could bear. He headed to the barn where he could be alone to sort through his feelings. It was good to see Alice again, and yet the memories and the pain tore unmercifully at his heart. He gasped for breath, with the awful pain. Then he heard a movement behind him.

"Luke?"

It was Jessie. "Luke, I know you want to be alone, but I can't leave you alone. Please, Brother, talk to me."

"I can't talk, Jessie," answered Luke, pounding the barn stall with his fist. "I just want this awful pain to go away. Did I make a mistake in coming back here? I can't deal with this."

"No," Jessie said emphatically. "Coming home was not a mistake. You are with people who love you. Paw messed up all our lives, Luke, but we can't let him win. We have to make something good of our lives. Maw deserves that. We all deserve it. I don't know what lies ahead, but we will face it together. Now take some time, then come on back in. Alice will be hurt if she thinks she has caused you more pain."

Luke turned away. "Jessie, I just don't know if I can stand to come back. All I can see is what might have been."

"Then let's do what you did with me the other day," said Jessie. "Let's pray."

Right there in the barn the two brothers prayed once more together.

"Looks like this is getting to be a habit," Luke said with a weak laugh. "Just give me a few minutes and I'll be back in. Okay, Brother?"

Jessie strolled back toward the house, feeling sad for his brother, yet at peace. *There might just be something to this prayer thing,* he thought to himself. Then he began to whistle.

As he rejoined them on the front porch, he heard Ady Rose ask Alice, "Are you doing okay, Alice? Do you have friends ... a good job?"

"I'm doing alright," answered Alice. "I live with an elderly lady and take care of her when I'm not at the hotel. She's very good to me."

"Have you thought of coming back here?" asked Belinda. "You would have a family if you moved back."

"I've thought about it every day since I left," replied Alice. "I'm afraid it would just be too hard on all of us. There are good memories, but so many bad ones. I'm not sure I could deal with them ... or if Luke could."

Carrie reached over and patted her hand. They were all sitting quietly as Luke walked back in. Then, one by one, each decided it was time to go home. First, Ady Rose and her family, followed by Belinda, Joe and little Cammy and then Nate took his leave.

"Well," said Cindy, somewhat ceremoniously, "I have things to do to prepare for tomorrow, so if you will excuse me...."

"And I have some animals to feed," said Jessie, rising from his chair.

"Then I will get to the kitchen for some chores," said Carrie. "I will speak with you again before you leave, Alice."

When all had taken their leave, Alice and Luke sat quietly, as if in deep thought.

Then Alice broke the silence. "Luke, I'm sorry to have surprised you like this. I guess I just didn't know any other way to do it. Will it ever get easier for us ... being together?"

Luke smiled, but the smile stopped just short of his eyes. "I don't know if it will ever get easier being together, Alice, but I know it will never get any easier being apart. It is good to see you. I think about you all the time."

"And I you," she responded. "Do you have anyone, Luke? A girl, I mean?"

Luke shook his head. "No. There's never been anyone. I guess it wasn't the same for you. I know you got married and had a child."

Alice winced at his words. "Yes, Luke, I was married for a few years, but it wasn't for love."

"Then why?" asked Luke. "Why did you marry?"

She settled back in her chair.

"When I left here, Luke, I had no one. I did get a job at a hotel much like the one in Haymaker. I lived with an older man and his wife, and they were very good to me. Ida, the woman, was ill with an incurable illness. Her husband took good care of her and I helped in any way I could. When she died, I didn't know what to do. I had nowhere to go, and yet it would have been inappropriate for me to stay on at the house. That's when Walter offered an idea. He asked me to marry him. He said I would have a home, and after he was gone it would be mine. We knew at the time he had a heart problem and would need someone to care for him eventually. So, I said yes. We were married two weeks after his wife died. It was a marriage of convenience, as they are called. I never loved him, although I cared for him, and I think his feelings were the same."

"But you had a child," said Luke, trying not to accuse.

"Yes, we had a child," whispered Alice. "She was the joy of my life and the jewel of his old age. Walter was twenty-five years older than me. Her name was Olivia ... and she was the most beautiful little angel I had ever seen. She was the little girl you and I should have had. God forgive me, Luke, I even pretended sometimes that she was yours. Then, like everything else, she was taken from me. I put her to bed one night, and when I got up in the night to check on her, her little body was cold. There was no breath. I buried her, and two months later, I buried her father."

With this, the tears came. Luke knelt by her chair and took her hands in his.

"My darling Alice," he said, "I wish I could take your pain. You have suffered so much in your life. If God is a God of love, why does He allow these things to happen?"

"I don't know, Luke," she answered, shaking her head from side to side. "But I do believe in His love. I don't understand it, but I believe in it. That's all that keeps me going sometimes."

Luke moved closer, taking her into his arms. It was the most wonderful feeling in the world.

"Alice, we could still get married," he urged. "We don't have to have children. I can live without anything else if I just have you."

She pulled quickly from his arms. "No, Luke. I can never marry you. I do love you, but we can never marry. You need to find someone that you can have a life and children with. I want that for you, Luke. I truly do."

"I can never offer my heart to someone else," said Luke. "My heart will always belong to you."

"Then I have truly ruined your life. May God forgive me."

With this, she arose quickly from her chair and headed toward the door. "Please say goodbye to Aunt Carrie for me."

Having heard the door slam, Carrie came into the living room to find Luke sitting in a chair, head in hands. When he looked up, she saw the same anguish she had seen years before when Lily had revealed the truth behind Alice's birth. She walked over, knelt down and took him into her arms.

"Oh, Luke," she said. "I wish I could spare you and Alice this pain. What happened to make her leave so suddenly?"

"I was stupid, Maw," he answered. "I was just pure old stupid. The first time I've seen her in years, and what do I do? I ask her to marry me. Stupid! Stupid!"

"No, my dear boy," said Carrie. "You are not stupid. But, Luke, you have to let her go. The marriage can never be, and your head knows that. It's your heart that won't let go. Alice realizes it can never be, but I'm sure it causes her the same pain that you are feeling."

"I don't want anyone to have this kind of pain," said Luke.

"I know, son. I know," soothed his mother.

The next day Carrie set out early toward Haymaker. She had to see Alice before she left town. She couldn't let her go without saying goodbye, and as she arrived in town, she headed toward the hotel. Syrena was at the desk, some paperwork in her hands. Her face held an unusual sadness.

"Good morning, Miss Carrie," she said, trying to smile. "What brings you here today? You usually don't work until Tuesday. I hope nothing is wrong."

"Oh, my dear," sighed Carrie. "Nothing and everything is wrong. Is Belinda here ... or more importantly, is Alice here?"

"Yes, to both," Syrena answered, looking quickly back at her paperwork. "They are in the sitting room. I think Alice is planning to leave."

Carrie headed toward the sitting room. "Thank you, dear."

Then she suddenly paused and looked back. "Syrena, just have patience. Can you do that?"

Syrena looked up with questioning eyes. Then she smiled. "Yes. I can be very patient, Miss Carrie. Thank you."

As Carrie entered the sitting room, Belinda sat on the sofa holding a tearful Alice's hand. She looked up to see her mother.

"Maw, what are you doing here today, and so early?"

"I had to come see Alice," Carrie replied. "Alice, Luke told me what happened. He's so sorry he upset you."

"It's not his fault, Aunt Carrie," Alice said, wiping her eyes. "I should never have come. I should have written to you to tell you about Homer and Belle."

"And missed out on holding your niece?" asked Carrie, smiling gently. "Just think of the joy it brought just to know who she is and to be able to hold her. I have found, dear, that no matter how bad the situation, God always brings some good into it. So don't be sorry you came. It was all in God's plan. But Alice...why must you go so soon?"

"My staying will just bring more heartache," said Alice. "Hasn't there been enough of that?"

"Your staying could also bring some peace," said Carrie. "Have you ever thought of that? Running from our problems is never a good solution."

"I don't know," said Alice, her voice quivering. "I get so lonely with no family. I must go back, but maybe I'll return soon. Maybe with a little time,

Luke and I can truly come to terms with the situation and be friends. Do you think that is possible?"

Putting her arms around Alice, Carrie said, "Yes, dear, I do. I think it is very possible. Besides, you will want to see your niece ... maybe even watch her grow up?"

Carrie and Belinda walked Alice to the train station and said goodbye. Though there was still sadness, their hearts were a little lighter with the expectation of a return and better days ahead. As Alice waved goodbye, there were tears, but there was also a smile. Perhaps ... just perhaps ... she would find a place to belong.

CHAPTER 12

Carrie feared that Luke would go into the abyss of depression, or maybe even leave again. But when she returned home he was gone, leaving a note that said,

> *Did all the necessary farm work. Going to check on the mercantile, then to the hotel to invite a lovely young lady to have lunch with me. Don't worry, Maw.*

Well, what do you make of that, thought Carrie. *A lovely young lady. Syrena? Oh, I hope so.*

Jessie came home for lunch, an unusual occurrence, and Carrie knew he must be worried. She hurried to get him a nice meal on the table. It had been quite some time since just the two of them had eaten lunch together.

"Looks good, Maw," he said, sitting down in his usual place. "I just thought you and me both might need a little company today. I wondered if Luke might be here, but I saw him in town. I was a little surprised at his mood. He was almost … happy, I guess you would say. He had been working at the mercantile all morning, according to Mandy, and whistling as he worked. I asked him if he wanted to come home with me to eat, but he said he had a date. I didn't know what he was talking about, but Mandy filled me in. It seems he asked Syrena to have lunch with him. Now what do you make of that?"

Maw smiled. "I don't know what to make of it, Jessie, but I choose to believe that it's a good sign. He and Alice can never be, but he and Syrena can. I would love to see him settled down with a good woman and a family ... just as I would like for you. I could use some more grandchildren to spoil, you know."

Jessie chose to ignore the last part of her statement. "He could sure do worse than Syrena, and it's plain to see that she likes him."

"And it's plain to see that Mandy likes you," said Carrie, not about to let him ignore her comment. "I also think it's plain that you like her. So what's holding you back, son?"

Jessie remained silent for a moment, and Carrie could tell he was considering his answer.

"Maw, I just don't think I could make any woman happy. What if I'm like Paw? What if I make her as miserable as Paw made all of us? What if I'm evil like he was, Maw?"

"Oh, Jessie," she answered, "you don't have an evil bone in your body."

"But I do," he insisted. "I think we both know that I do."

Carrie reached out and took his hand. "Is there something you need to talk about, my boy? You know you can tell me anything and I'll always love you. Nothing you could ever say or do would stop my love. It is unconditional. Don't you know that?"

Once more he sat in silence, all thoughts of eating gone. Tears began to slide down his cheeks.

"Maw, we never talked about Paw's death."

"Do we need to talk about it?" she asked. "Do you want to tell me what happened that day? Remember, nothing will change my love."

He continued to sit in silence, unable to speak.

Finally, Carrie could stand it no longer. "Jessie, did you kill your Paw?"

The intake of his breath was almost frightening, but still he couldn't speak.

"Just start at the beginning, son, and tell me. No one is here but you and me. It's time, Jessie. It's time."

Jessie raised his head and looked at her. The wretched torment hooding his eyes was almost more than she could bear.

"I saw Paw in town that day," he began. "He didn't see me, but I saw him, and I knew he was up to no good because he was supposed to be at work. He was headed to that little cove just a ways from Mattie and Charlie Lawson's house, and I had no doubt he was going there to meet a woman, so I followed him. Oh, the hate I was feeling in my heart, Maw."

At this, Carrie reached her other hand out until she was holding both his hands, as if to give him strength for what he must tell her.

"It didn't take long to see that I was right. He met her and I heard her tell him they should go down by the river. Of course, I followed them. I could tell Paw was frustrated at having to go so far. I could hear them talking.

What is so dad-blamed important that we have to come all the way to the river? What's on your mind, woman?

You always liked to be with me before, Tom. Don't you like to be with me no more?

Paw seemed to calm down some when she said that, and he reached out to take her hand.

Okay, sweetheart, what has got you upset? Is it that paw of yours?

No, Tom. It ain't him. Tom, I hope you'll be happy about this and not be mad. Tom, I'm ... going to have your baby.

I could see Paw turn white. He looked like he was about to fall over ... and then a change came over him. I saw the same rage in his eyes I used to see when he was mad at Luke or me. We always knew what was coming.

What are you talking about, woman? My baby? Why, if you are with child, there's no telling who it belongs to. Don't you think you're gonna come whining to me and expect me to give you money. It ain't gonna happen!

But, Tom, the woman said, catching at his shirt sleeve. *Tom, I know it's yours. You told me I was special. You told me it was the best time of your life when you could be with me. I love you, Tom. I don't want you to give me money. I want you to marry me!*

I've never seen Paw's face so angry ... not even the times he got mad at us. Before I knew what was happening, he drew back his hand and belted her on the side of the head, and she went flying a few feet and then hit the ground. I wanted to run out and stop him but I couldn't get my feet to move. To my shame, I just stood behind the bushes and watched.

Don't you ever come at me with that nonsense again, Paw roared. *I have a wife and family and you're nothing but a cheap floozy who'll sell herself to any man that comes along. Don't you come near me again and don't you speak of this to anyone or you'll be sorry you did.*

With this, Paw spat on the ground and went stomping away. The woman raised up from the ground where she had fallen, and she suddenly had this look of hatred and rage. She picked up a large rock lying near her. She silently followed Paw, and when she was close enough she hit him in the back of the head with the rock. Paw fell to the ground with a thud, and she went running away crying.

"Oh, Jessie," cried Carrie, "that must have been so horrible for you to see. But, son, that means you didn't kill your father. Right?"

"I don't know," he replied.

"What do you mean you don't know?" asked Carrie. "You just said she hit Tom with a big rock and he fell to the ground. How could you have killed him?"

"I went over to his body," said Jessie, quietly. "I didn't know I could hate someone like I hated him at that moment. I took my foot and pushed him over. I stared at that ugly, mean face that had caused so much misery to so many people. Then I pushed him again ... and again ... and again ... until he was in the river. Then I gave him another push with my foot until he was all the way out in the water. He was face down, just sort of floating but going nowhere. I thought to myself, *I can't see his face now. I won't ever have to look at that evil face again. He will never hurt Maw again.* Then I turned around and went back to town.

For a moment, silence prevailed between mother and son, until Jessie spoke again.

"I don't know if I killed him, Maw. I never even checked to see if he was alive or dead before I shoved him into the water. So what does that make me? I don't know if I murdered him, but I know murder was in my heart."

Carrie put her arms around him and rocked him back and forth like she had when he was a child. She cried for her son and the torment he had been forced to live with.

Why didn't I leave Tom, she asked herself. *I could have prevented all of this suffering. May God forgive me.*

"Does anyone else know about this?" she asked.

Jessie nodded. "Yes. I told Sheriff Ashton the week after the funeral. He went back to the riverbank and examined the evidence. He said it was something we would probably never know for sure, but it was his opinion that Paw was already dead before I pushed him into the river. He asked me who the woman was, but I refused to tell him. I saw no reason for anyone else to suffer for Paw's evil ways. I watched and waited for several months, but she never had a baby. I don't know if she wasn't really with child or if she lost it. I just thank God that another child wasn't brought into this world to suffer for what Paw did."

"Then I won't even ask you who she was, Jessie," said Carrie. "I believe Sheriff Ashton told you what he truly believed. He wasn't a man to lie or sugar-coat things. Now, you must let it go. I understand the hate you felt, son. Though I never let it show, there were times when I hated Tom."

"You, Maw?" gasped Jessie. "I don't believe you could ever hate anyone."

"Not for what he did to me," said Carrie, shaking her head, "but a mother can hate for her children. I hated the misery he caused for all of you. I hated him for the look he caused in your eyes and Luke's eyes. Yes, my darling boy, a mother can hate for her children, and there were many times I could have picked up a rock and hit him. Jessie, if anyone deserves to bear the guilt, it's me. No mother should ever put up with what I did, allowing her children to be hurt to the point that they feel such hate. I was wrong, son. I was wrong."

"No, Maw," said Jessie. "You were always our refuge, and you taught us what love is all about, but thank you for telling me all this. I don't understand why, but it helps me to know that you felt that way."

After a few moments of quiet, Jessie spoke again. "Maw, there's one more person I have to tell about that day."

"Luke?"

"Yes. He knows something is wrong, but he doesn't know what. He deserves to know the truth."

Carrie squeezed his hand. "Then tell him, Jessie ... and soon. Now, go on with your life, son. Put this in the past. Maybe we both have had to deal with some hate, but we won't let that cripple us. You will make a fine husband and father because you have learned from your experience how important that is."

Jessie hugged his mother and left to go back to work. Carrie smiled as he walked down the hill. She could almost swear he had a lightness to his step, and she didn't know why, but she felt different inside. It was as if she had finally closed a door ... and although she couldn't understand it, somehow she knew there was another door for her to open.

CHAPTER 13

Christmas could only be described as light and joyful. Everyone was in such gleeful spirits, laughing, joking ... and being a little bit sneaky about some things. Jessie and Mandy had been seeing each other regularly and his mother and sisters whispered to each other, "It's only a matter of time?"

Leah and Nathan were filled with the Christmas excitement that only children can know, and little Cammy was just learning to walk as she garbled out all kinds of sounds that her parents insisted were words. Carrie just sat back, watched and smiled in her newfound peace and contentment. She was also noticing something about the look on Ady Rose's face ... a glow.

If that glow means what I think it means.... she thought smugly. *Oh, I hope so.*

On Christmas day they were all together, including Nate, Mandy and Syrena. Everyone was trying to keep Cammy from crawling to the tree and tearing at the presents. Well, almost everyone. Luke and Jessie seemed to be encouraging her just a little.

"When can we open presents?" asked Nathan, bobbing up and down.

"Not until after dinner, Nathan," answered Leah, in her big sister voice. "Didn't you hear what Mama said before we left home?"

With this Nathan stuck his tongue out at his sister, leading to a quick reprimand from his dad.

"Whatever are we going to do with these two?" asked Ady Rose. "Well, Willy, do you think this would be a good time to tell our news?"

"I think it would," replied Willy, with a huge smile.

"We're going to have a baby!" they both shouted together.

"Oh, I just knew it!" exclaimed Carrie.

Ady Rose looked at her in disbelief. "You knew it, Maw? Who told you?"

"No one had to tell me," laughed Carrie. "You just had that glow. Now when is my grandchild due?"

"About the first of May," answered Ady Rose. "We're going to have a springtime baby."

"I hope it's a boy," declared Cindy.

"Why do you hope that?" asked Ady Rose.

Smiling, Cindy answered, "Because Nathan is outnumbered around here. Right, Nathan?"

"Right, Aunt Cindy," he said with the biggest of smiles.

"I don't mean to change the subject," said Carrie, "but I have some news everyone might be interested in."

"What news is that, Maw?" asked Jessie. "I hope you're not with child!"

At this everyone broke into laughter ... everyone except Carrie.

Smacking Jessie on the arm, she replied, "Watch your mouth young man. I still know where the soap is."

"No! No! Not the dreaded soap, Maw!" exclaimed Jessie, sitting in Luke's lap. "Save me, Brother! Save me!"

"Okay, now. Enough." Carrie reprimanded. "Be still so I can tell my news. I had a letter from Clay this week."

"And how is our long-lost baby brother?" questioned Luke.

"He is well ... and he is married," answered Carrie.

"Married?" they all exclaimed.

"When did this happen, Maw?" asked Ady Rose. "Why didn't he invite his own family?"

Pulling out a white envelope, Carrie said, "Let me just read you what he says."

Dear Maw,

I'm sorry I haven't written much lately, but it's been a busy time. First of all, I am now a married man. Abigail and I were married the week before Thanksgiving. I would have invited all of you, but I knew it would be hard for you to get here, especially near the holiday. We have a new home on Mr. McCleary's ranch and we are very happy. She is a wonderful woman, Maw, and I know you will love her. I can't wait for you to meet her, and you will get that chance in April, as we are coming home for a few days, if that is alright with you. I will let you know the exact date of our arrival a little later on. In the meantime, it will mean a lot to me to have your blessing. Give my love to the rest of the family.

Yours affectionately,

Clay

"Hard for us to get there!" exclaimed Ady Rose. "Has my brother never heard of trains?"

Patting his wife on the shoulder, Willy said, "Now don't get yourself in a huff, Ady Rose. I'm sure Clay had little to do with the wedding plans."

"It looks like Abigail would have wanted Clay's family at her wedding," said Belinda.

"Children," said Carrie, "I don't know why we weren't invited, but I choose to look at the part where he says they will be home in April. It has been so long since I've seen my youngest son, and my heart longs for his arrival. I'm sure Abigail is a pleasant young woman or Clay would not have chosen her. Now, let's just look forward to April ... and in the meantime, let's eat so we can open presents."

As they gathered around the table, everyone became quiet, knowing that their meals always began with someone saying grace. They all looked at Maw.

"Nate," she said, looking across the table, "would you please say grace over our Christmas meal?"

After a few covert winks around the table, they all bowed their heads.

The meal was a festive occasion, with laughter, kidding and reminiscing. Afterward, they all settled in the living room and Maw picked up the family Bible.

"Jessie, would you read the Christmas story this year?" she asked.

Their eyes met and Jessie's held a questioning look. Then he smiled.

"I would love to read the story, Maw." And that was what he did.

Afterward, presents were given out by Willy and Joe. The children were filled with excitement and were quick to show their appreciation for every gift. Maw had made Leah and Nathan each a new coat and they were thrilled. She had made a beautiful quilt covered in farm animals for Cammy. But the gift that received the most attention was the gift Nate gave to Carrie. It was the last one handed out.

Picking up the small box, Joe read, "To Carrie, From Nate."

All was silent as Carrie removed the paper and opened the box.

"Ohhh!" she gasped. "It's beautiful!"

In the box was the loveliest of cameo brooches. It was black with sparkling white etching and trimmed with an intricate silver design.

"Uncle Nate, you sure know how to pick a gift," declared Cindy.

The look on Carrie's face was priceless. "Thank you, Nate. I don't know that I've ever had a nicer present."

"You deserve it, Carrie," he answered. "And it's no lovelier than the lady who will be wearing it."

Carrie's face was beet-red from the compliment, and she did not see the smiles on the faces of her children.

It was a special Christmas ... one the family would never forget.

The winter proved to be a mild one and Carrie continued to work at the hotel and dress shop on Tuesdays and Wednesdays, spending part of that time with her granddaughter. Cammy grew and thrived with all the love showered on her and was now walking on her own. Luke had purchased a new car a few months back, and he could drive Carrie to work if the roads were not too bad. More and more people in the community were buying cars, and they were becoming a common sight. The town had even purchased a police car for Jessie. Carrie remembered that Henry Hankins had been one of the first to own a car, and she remembered how jealous Tom was of him. Henry and Lizzie had lived across the road from Carrie many years now and had become good neighbors. Lizzie seemed to have left her previous life behind her.

It was a Wednesday and Carrie was working in the little dress shop, sewing the lace on a new dress she and Syrena had been making. She was becoming quite fond of Syrena and was happy that Luke had taken her out several times. It was plain to see how Syrena felt about him. As Carrie worked, she hummed, but the humming was suddenly interrupted by a loud siren. At first she thought of the mines, but Belinda came running into the room to look out the window.

"It's the fire siren!" she exclaimed. "Oh, I hope it's nothing bad."

The siren continued and crowds were gathering in the streets. As they looked out the window, the women could see smoke rising to the east toward the outskirts of town.

Suddenly they heard shouting. "It's the schoolhouse! It's the schoolhouse!"

"Oh no," cried Carrie. "Cindy! Cindy's at school!"

"Now, Miss Carrie, I'm sure Cindy's alright," said Syrena, putting her arm around Carrie.

About that time, Joe came running through the door.

"Joe, is it the school?" asked Belinda. "Do you know if anyone is hurt?"

Catching his breath, Joe nodded. "It is the school, but everyone is out and okay."

"What happened? Do you know?" Carrie asked. "Where is Cindy?"

"Now, Maw Carrie, don't get excited," said Joe. "Cindy is with the kids. You know she would never leave them. It does look like the school is a complete loss, though. Don't know what caused it, but Jessie and Luke are over there, so I'm sure they will give us the lowdown when they can. Let's just be thankful no one was hurt."

It was a good two hours later when Jessie, Luke and Cindy arrived at the hotel, looking tired and black with soot. Cindy was in tears.

"Oh, Maw!" she cried. "Our school is gone! What will we do without our school?"

"It will be alright, dear one," soothed Carrie. "No one was hurt. That's the important thing. A school can be rebuilt, but the loss of a life can't be undone."

Things quieted down in the streets as everyone returned home. Carrie took her leave from the hotel as she felt Cindy needed to get home and rest. Jessie had to go back to the scene to help determine the cause of the fire, but Luke drove the women home. He assured Jessie he would return to help in any way he was needed. Later, as both returned, Carrie and Cindy were waiting to hear what news they had.

"We think the fire started around the chimney," said Jessie. "Don't know exactly why."

"Do you think the town will build a new school?" asked Cindy.

"I'm sure they will, Cindy," replied Jessie, "but that will take time and money. There's no way they can have one ready before next fall, if then."

"But what about the children?" asked Cindy, eyes welling with tears. "They'll get behind in their education. Isn't there any place in town we could set up a school ... maybe an empty building?"

"I'm sure something will be worked out, little sister," said Luke. "It just happened and everyone needs time to think. Why don't you and Maw get to bed and get some rest. Tomorrow will be another day and we'll all be thinking more clearly."

Luke and Jessie sat pondering as the women went to bed. Finally, Jessie spoke.

"What Cindy said about an empty building made me think, Luke."

"You know of one?" asked Luke.

"Maybe," Jessie answered. "What about the Ashton house? They left it to me, and some day I may live in it, but I have no plans for that now. Do you think that might work? Do you think the town council would go for the idea?"

Luke's eyes lit up. "I sure do like the idea, and I have a feeling they just might. But what about a blackboard and desks and books?"

"Well, we'll just have to tackle each problem one by one," said Jessie. "Let's don't mention it to Cindy until we know more. Okay?"

"Agreed," said Luke. "Now I think this old boy is ready for bed."

CHAPTER 14

A week later the town council voted to use the Ashton house as a temporary school. They also voted to buy a blackboard that could later be installed in a new school. There was not enough money for desks and books, so they voted to buy books, as they also could be used later. A church that had closed over in Collins offered to sell the town some backless pews at a cheap price, so they voted to buy those and wait to invest in desks.

Cindy was elated when Luke and Jessie told her that night.

"We can start having school again!" she cried. "Oh, thank you, Jessie, for letting us use the house. I know Mr. and Mrs. Ashton would be pleased."

Before they knew it April was being ushered in with daffodils and hyacinths. Winter had been mild and it looked like spring would come early. Only one thing dampened the joy of a new spring. The second week in April Carrie received a letter from Clay. Luke found her sitting in her rocking chair at the window, holding the letter as tears traced a path down her pale cheeks.

He went to her and knelt down. "Maw, what is it? Is it bad news? Is it from Alice?"

"No, dear," she answered, placing her hand on his cheek. "I'm just being a silly old woman. Clay is not coming home. They have just found out Abigail is with child and she doesn't think it's a good idea to travel right now."

Luke took her hand in his. "I'm so sorry, Maw. I know how much you were looking forward to their visit. We all were. But it's a good thing, too. You're going to be a grandmother again. Isn't that a good thing?"

"Yes, it is," she laughed weakly. "It's a very good thing. But, Luke, do you think we will ever get to see the child?"

Luke didn't answer. He was afraid Maw wouldn't like the answer he had.

In May, school was out. It was bittersweet for Cindy, as she knew she would not be returning to teach in the fall. She was looking forward to going to the teacher's school in September, though. She and Maw had been busy making her some new dresses and making list after list of things she would need.

On a Sunday afternoon as everyone sat on the porch, talk abounded. Ady Rose and her family had not joined them as Ady Rose's baby was due any day now. As the ladies were deep in conversation, Luke asked Jessie to take a walk with him. They walked out the familiar little path, passing the barn, and stopped at the old split apple tree.

"Do you remember the night lightning hit this old tree?" asked Luke. "Split it right down the middle but didn't topple it. Never had apples on it again."

"Yeah, I remember," laughed Jessie. "Made Paw mad as all get-out, but he didn't know who to be mad at and that made him even madder. He wouldn't even cut the darn thing down because he wanted to stay mad at it."

They both laughed, and then were quiet ... until Luke spoke.

"Jessie, remember the day Mr. Lundy read Mr. Ashton's will and we were walking home? We said we wanted to do something good with what he left us."

"I remember," Jessie nodded. "That's one reason I offered the house for use as a school. It seemed that was one way it could be used for good."

"And it was good," said Luke. "I've been thinking about the money he left me and I think I know what I want to do with it. I want to build a new school, Jessie!"

"Why, Luke, that's a splendid idea!" cried Jessie. "That would definitely be using it for good."

Luke continued, "Jessie, I don't know if the town council will go along with this, but I don't want to build just a one-room school. I want some-

77

thing bigger, like maybe four or five rooms where the kids can go from first grade all the way through high school. Eight years of school just isn't enough anymore. What do you think?"

"I like it, Brother," Jessie answered. "It sounds like you've been doing quite a bit of thinking and looking into this."

Luke nodded. "I have. I think with the money Mr. Ashton left me, I could build the school, buy the desks and pay the teachers' salaries for one year. I just don't know if the town will be able to pay the teachers' salaries after that. We will need more books, too, and more blackboards."

"You won't know until you ask them," said Jessie. "Here's another thought: Maybe some of the others in town would like to donate money for books or blackboards."

"Yeah," said Luke. "I hadn't thought of that. Now let's not mention this to anyone until after the town council meeting. I don't want to get anyone's hopes up only to see them dashed."

Luke had no need to worry. The town council voted unanimously to accept his money to build a larger school. Several of the men admitted they had been talking about adding a high school for quite some time. Mr. Thacker, who owned the harness and furniture store in town, offered right then and there to donate money for all books needed. Phyllis Johnson, owner of the diner, vowed to donate the money for three more blackboards. Luke left the meeting with a happy heart.

Mr. Ashton, he thought, *I believe you would be happy with this. I am using it for good, just as you always did.*

Carrie and Cindy were thrilled beyond words when the boys brought home the news.

"I just hope I'll be able to teach at the new school," said Cindy. "Wouldn't that be just grand, Maw."

Carrie smiled and nodded. "Oh, indeed, it would! Indeed, it would!"

"It will take several months to build," said Luke, "and they won't be starting for at least a month, as plans have to be drawn up and carpenters have to be hired. There's a lot to be done, and we want this done right. Jessie has agreed to let them use the Ashton house until the new school is completely ready."

Thoughts of the new schoolhouse were set aside for awhile, as two days later Ady Rose finally went into labor. The baby was late and she had been miserable, but all it took was the beautiful loud wail of her new son to erase all the pain and waiting. Ethan William was a healthy baby, weighing in at 8 pounds and 11 ounces.

"Wow, sis, he's half grown," laughed Jessie.

"We grow 'em that way at our house," boasted Willie playfully.

Carrie just held the tiny finger of her new grandchild and smiled. *You just don't know what you have missed out on, Tom,* she thought.

The following Saturday night, everyone seemed to have plans, so Carrie and Nate were alone when he came over for supper. He bragged on everything Carrie had fixed, as he always did.

"Best apple pie in the land," he said, rubbing his stomach.

"I think you just say that so I'll keep making them," laughed Carrie.

They did the dishes together, talking as they washed and dried. *I can't imagine Tom ever washing or drying a dish,* thought Carrie, looking out the corner of her eye at Nate.

Later they sat on the front porch together in the rocking chairs.

"It sure is quiet with all the children gone," remarked Carrie. "I have a feeling inside of me that before long they will all be gone with their own lives, and it will just be me and this old house."

"I know about being alone," sighed Nate. "After Charlotte died, I began talking to the walls, I was so lonely. Of course, she had been sick for a long time and the last several months she wasn't even able to talk to me. I often regret that God didn't give us kids. I guess that's why I enjoy your kids so much, Carrie. They seem like the ones I never had."

"That's a nice thing for you to say, Nate," said Carrie. "I know they are all mighty fond of you."

From the corner of his eye, Nate looked at Carrie's hand on the arm of her rocker. Before he lost his nerve, he reached over and put his hand over hers, scared of what her reaction might be. To his surprise, she didn't draw her hand away, but kept on rocking. So Nate kept on rocking ... but he smiled.

Little Ethan grew and thrived as summer passed into fall. Cindy left the last week of August to meet the elderly lady she would be living with and to get settled in before her classes began. She was nervous, but excited, and Carrie was excited for her. She had no doubt that Cindy would do well and that she would bring something special to everyone she met.

Carrie kept busy with her own home, the dress shop and her grandchildren ... not to mention Nate, who was there every Saturday night and Sunday afternoon. The handholding had become a normal thing when they were alone, and though she said nothing, Carrie sort of liked it. Jessie and Mandy were seeing quite a lot of each other and Luke asked Syrena out from time to time. Everything seemed so peaceful ... but life has a way of shaking that peace.

It was a Friday afternoon in mid-September and Carrie was sitting on the front porch, mending some of Luke's and Jessie's shirts and socks. As she looked up from her work, she saw a young woman coming up the hill. She held her hand over her eyes to shade from the sun and then gasped. Alice!

As she neared the gate, Carrie arose from her chair. "Alice! It is so good to see you! What a surprise!"

As she topped the last step, Alice hugged Carrie. "I guess I always surprise everyone. I hope this is not a bad time."

"Oh, dear child," exclaimed Carrie. "There is no such thing as a bad time for seeing you. Now sit down and catch your breath. What brings you here? I hope nothing is wrong."

Alice looked away as she sat down, and Carrie had a feeling of foreboding.

"Isn't this beautiful fall weather?" asked Carrie.

"Yes," said Alice. "It definitely is, and there's no place as lovely as here in the fall. I don't think I could ever live in the city."

"Did you bring bags?" asked Carrie. "We would love to have you stay with us while you're here."

"No, Aunt Carrie," she answered. "I don't think it would be a good idea to stay here, although I appreciate you asking. I'm staying at the hotel. I got to town yesterday."

"Is anything wrong, dear?" asked Carrie, unable to hold back the question any longer.

"Yes, there is," said Alice, "but I would like to talk to you and Luke about it together, if you don't mind."

"With Luke?" questioned Carrie, before she thought. "I'm sorry, Alice. Of course, we can wait until Luke is here."

80

"There is something you can help me with, though, Aunt Carrie."

Carrie reached out and took her hand. "Anything, dear heart. All you have to do is ask."

"I want you to go with me to see Lily," said Alice.

Carrie drew in her breath, completely taken by surprise. "You want to go see Lily?"

"Yes," nodded Alice. "There's something I must say to her. I have to tell her that I forgive her."

For a moment Carrie was unable to speak. "I don't understand, Alice. It's a good thing that you have forgiven her, but what has brought all of this on?"

"I just need to let her know that I have forgiven her," reiterated Alice. "It may not mean anything to her, but it's something I must do. Will you go with me?"

"Of course, I'll go," said Carrie. "When do you want to go?"

"Tomorrow, if it's convenient for you," answered Alice. "I would like to stay here until Luke gets home and talk with both of you, then go see Lily tomorrow."

Carrie was completely confused, but tried not to show it. They spent the rest of the afternoon just catching up on all the news. At five o'clock Luke came home, utterly surprised to find Alice there. Carrie was proud of the way he handled the situation. He was flustered, she knew, but was completely calm as he greeted her.

"Jessie says to tell you not to hold supper for him, Maw," he said. "It seems he is taking the lovely Mandy out for supper."

"Are Jessie and Mandy getting serious?" asked Alice.

"It would seem that way," answered Luke. "I think my little brother has been bitten by that old love bug."

"Luke, Alice has come to talk to you and me about something," said Carrie. "I think we'll hold supper awhile and let her talk. I have a feeling she needs to get this out. Am I right, Alice?"

"Yes," said Alice. "You always could read me like a book, Aunt Carrie."

"Then just talk, darling, and we'll listen."

Carrie and Luke sat silently, waiting for Alice to speak. It took her a few moments, but finally she cleared her throat and began.

"First of all, I am back here to stay," she began. "Belinda has given me a room at the hotel, and in payment I will work there and in the dress shop as long as I can."

Luke stared at her for a moment, trying to see beneath her words. "What do you mean, *as long as you can?*" He held his breath, knowing that the answer was not going to be something he wanted to hear.

"I-I have something wrong with me," she stammered. "I have known for quite some time something was wrong, but I put off going to the doctor, hoping the problem would go away. But it didn't ... so I went to a clinic. The doctors say I have something growing inside of me ... and I won't get well."

"You mean...." gasped Carrie.

"Yes, Aunt Carrie," Alice said. "I'm dying."

"NO!" shouted Luke, jumping up from his chair. "I won't hear this. Don't say those words!"

Carrie tugged at his shirt sleeve. "Luke, sit down! You are not doing Alice any good this way. We need to listen to her. She needs to tell us."

Luke, a ghostly white, took his seat as though in a haze.

"I know this is hard to hear," continued Alice. "It was hard for me to hear when the doctors told me two months ago and it's hard for me to tell you."

"Two months ago!" gasped Carrie. "Child, have you been living with this knowledge all by yourself for two months?"

"Yes, but I needed that time to come to terms with it all," answered Alice. "Then I knew I must come and tell the people I love most."

"H-how much time d-do the doctors say you have?" asked Luke.

"Six months ... maybe a year," she answered so quietly they could hardly hear her.

They all sat in silence as Carrie and Luke tried to digest all that she had just revealed.

Carrie spoke, "Alice, you cannot stay in a hotel room. I want you to pack your belongings and come here to stay. You will need someone to take care of you."

"I can't do that, Aunt Carrie. Please understand. It would be too hard for Luke and for me. I just can't stay here."

"Then I'll leave," said Luke. "I can stay in town in back of the mercantile and you can stay here."

82

"No, Luke," answered Alice emphatically. "I need you both to respect my wishes. If things change and I see I can't stay there, then I will reconsider, but not now. At this point it will be much easier on me physically to live where I will be working."

Carrie rose from her chair. "I think the two of you need to talk, so I will go fix us some supper. You can come in when you're ready."

When Carrie was inside the house, Luke moved over to the chair next to Alice, but he did not try to take her hand.

"Alice, I promise to respect your wishes," he said gently. "I also promise to be there for you whenever you need me, but don't shut me out. This is something I need to see you through, probably more for my sake than for yours. Can you let me do that, Alice?"

"Yes," she replied. "I will gladly accept your help. I need your help. And Luke...while you and I can never be as we had planned, I have never stopped loving you. But can we now try to love each other as friends? That's what I need now, Luke. I need your love, but also your understanding of the limits."

"I can be anything you want me to be," said Luke, finally reaching out to take her hand.

Soon they went in to supper, although no one ate much. She and Carrie made plans to visit Lily the following day, and Luke let them talk without his input. Afterward, Luke drove Alice back to the hotel. Driving home he felt a million hands clutching at his throat, stifling his breathing little by little. He had to pull over to the side of the road.

"God!" he cried out. "Why? Why are you doing this? What has Alice ever done in her life but love others and take care of them? She is a beautiful soul, God. Why? Why?"

His body shook with uncontrollable sobs. Then, when the sobs would come no more, a peace crept over him ... a peace he did not understand. But with this peace came a determination ... a determination to make Alice's last days as happy as he could possibly make them. *God*, he whispered, *help me to forget about myself, my wants, my needs, and to be what I need to be for Alice. Help me to make her time left a peaceful and happy time. I need you, God, as I've never needed you before.*

When he reached home, he sat in Carrie's rocker, staring at the sky, just thinking. Carrie saw him there, but remained inside, praying for her son, as she knew he needed this time to himself. She also knew there were rough days ahead for him, but he would be okay. God would take care of him. She prayed, too, that Syrena would be alright through all of this, and selfishly she prayed that Syrena would wait for Luke.

The next day began with sunshine, something Carrie needed to get through this visit she would be making with Alice. It had been two years since she had even seen her sister Lily, and that had been briefly in the mercantile. She had no real desire to see her, but knew she must go for Alice's sake. She wondered what Lily's reaction would be to Alice and hoped she would say nothing to hurt her. People told her that Lily had changed and she hoped that was true. Alice needed peace in her life. Carrie wasn't sure she understood her need to see Lily, but then she had never faced what Alice was facing. *Let this bring peace and comfort to her, God.*

It was ten o'clock when she arrived at the hotel to meet Alice so they could walk to Lily's together. Syrena was at the desk, arranging some papers.

"Good morning, Syrena," she said. "I hope you are feeling well this sunny morning."

Syrena looked up and Carrie saw the sadness in her eyes. She was just about to say something when Alice came into the room. Syrena quickly looked back down at the papers.

Coming to hug her aunt, Alice smiled, "Good morning, Aunt Carrie. Are you ready for this?"

"Well, I hope I am," said Carrie. "Alice, are you sure about this? If my sister hurts you I may have to show my temper."

"Do you have a temper?" asked Alice, laughing. "I don't think I've ever seen you even in a bad mood. But, yes, I am ready. I have no expectations except to let her know I harbor no hard feelings. What she does with that knowledge is up to her. Shall we go?"

As they walked toward the door, Alice turned to Syrena. "Syrena, I promise to be back in time to put the lace on that blue dress for Mrs. Wilmer."

Syrena smiled and nodded.

They walked at a carefree pace from the hotel to Lily's house. Alice even seemed happy. Without hesitation, she knocked at the door, and it was only a few seconds before the door was opened. Carrie didn't know what she had expected, but it was not what she saw before her. Was this even her sister? Lily had aged beyond description, her hair completely gray, her skin pallid and sagging. The mischief that had once been in her eyes was replaced by a dullness. The change almost took her breath away. She looked sideways at Alice and could see the same response, but Alice quickly recovered with a bright smile on her face.

"Good morning, Lily," she said. "I hope you don't mind that we came by without asking first."

Lily stood as though in a daze.

"Lily, are you okay?" asked Carrie.

Finally gathering her wits, Lily opened the door wider. "Alice? Carrie? You are the last two people I expected to see on my doorstep, but please, come in. I'm a little taken back, but I'm glad to see you both."

They entered the living room, which was worn, but neat. Alice and Carrie sat on the sofa as Lily sat in the chair across from them. Carrie couldn't help but reflect that even the house seemed to have lost its vigor.

"Alice, how have you been?" asked Lily. "It's been a long time."

"Yes, it has," replied Alice. "A lot has happened since we last met, and we didn't part on the best of terms. That's why I'm here, Lily."

"Wh-what do you mean," questioned Lily. "Alice, I regret what I had to do that day and the pain it caused you. All of you," she added, looking at Carrie. "I did it because I felt I had to. I couldn't let you marry your brother. Don't you see?"

"I'm here to tell you I bear no hard feelings toward you, Lily," said Alice, smiling. "That is my entire reason for being here. I want there to be peace between us."

Even more color drained from Lily's already pale cheeks. "I can't believe it," she said. "I never thought you would want to see me again, much less forgive me. What has brought this change in you, Alice?"

"I guess years of living and losing have made me see the importance of relationships," answered Alice. "A lot has happened in the past years. I married; I had a child. I lost the child and then her father. I have known pain and loss and I have found that I have no energy for hate and bitterness. I don't know why all of these things have happened in my life, but I believe in God's holy plan, and He says that we are to forgive."

Tears streamed from Lily's cheeks and she did not even try to wipe them away. "I don't know if you can believe me or not, but I've changed. Carrie, you know how wild and wanton I've been all my life. I don't know why.

Mama and Papa didn't raise me to be that way. It just seemed like the devil got in me and I couldn't get him out ... didn't even want to get him out. I told everyone I gave my children away because I couldn't take care of them, but that wasn't the truth. I was selfish, and I just wanted the world to be wrapped around me. I wanted men to admire me and want me. But, you know what? Even with all the partying and drinking ... and yes, men ... I was never happy. None of that made me happy, but I just couldn't stop."

"What made you change?" asked Carrie, unable to hide the doubt in her voice.

"Well, to be absolutely honest," answered Lily, "I started getting tired of it all. I don't know if it was because I was getting older that brought it about, or if I just got bored with it all? I'm being absolutely honest with you now. I'm just not sure when the change began ... but then one day I received a letter."

"A letter?" asked Alice. "From who?"

More tears ran down Lily's face. "It was from Belle," she finally rasped, and then broke into sobs.

Without even hesitating, Alice knelt down at her chair and took her hand. She waited for Lily to be able to continue.

"Belle was married," said Lily, finally. "She said she didn't know if I would even care, but she wanted me to know she had been adopted by two wonderful people and she had had a good childhood. She said that giving her up was probably the best thing I could have done for her."

With this, Lily broke into more sobs. Alice continued to hold her hand.

"Her adoptive parents died when she was eighteen, she said. She didn't say how they died. Then she told me she had met a wonderful, God-fearing man and they had married and that she was extremely happy. At the time that she wrote her letter, she had just found out that she was going to have a baby. She said she wanted me to know, even if it didn't mean anything to me, that I was going to be a-a gr-grandmother."

Now Lily was sobbing uncontrollably and Alice sat quietly holding her hand, knowing that the tears were necessary. They were washing away the shame and guilt and loss.

Finally, as the tears began to subside, Alice spoke. "I am glad she wrote to you, Lily. I searched for her for years, but found her too late."

"What do you mean by *too late*?" asked Lily, looking at the young woman before her.

"Belle died two weeks after her baby was born," said Alice quietly.

"Died?" said Lily, as though she couldn't quite wrap her mind around the word. "But why? How?"

"I don't know the details," replied Alice. "I know that the husband, who was also an orphan, took the baby to raise, but a short time later he was killed in a logging accident. The baby was given up for adoption."

Alice stopped here with the story. She did not feel it was her right to tell Lily who adopted the baby.

"But for a short time she was happy," said Lily, as if saying those words brought some comfort. She continued, "Receiving that letter seemed to change my whole life. For the first time, I saw what I was ... what I had always been ... and I didn't want to be that person anymore. I told Dent about all of it, and it seemed to change him, too. We don't party anymore. We are just content to stay here at the house."

"Have you thought about going to church?" asked Alice, quietly.

"If I walk into a church it would just start tongues to wagging," answered Lily. "I wouldn't blame them, but why cause problems in a church? I've caused enough people problems and heartache."

Alice didn't respond. Now was not the time.

Lily looked at her again. "I hope you can go on with your life and be happy. I know your life has had a lot of hurt, but you're still young. There's still time."

Alice and Carrie exchanged a glance, but neither said anything. Again, it was not the time. They left a short time later, accomplishing what they had gone there for, and even a little more. As they walked back to the hotel, they were quiet, each lost in her own thoughts. There would be time later for talking.

CHAPTER 15

A few days later, Carrie went to the hotel dress shop for her usual day of work and tending to Cammy. As she entered she heard laughter. No one was at the desk, so she followed the sound to the dress shop. What she saw made her gasp. There were Alice and Syrena sitting at the sewing table laughing as though they had been friends forever. Belinda came up beside her mother.

"Like you said, Maw ... God moves in mysterious ways," she whispered.

"What has brought this on?" asked Carrie.

Belinda motioned for her to follow her, so Carrie pulled her eyes from the amusing scene.

"What happened?" asked Carrie again. "I never thought I'd see those two laughing together."

"The other day when Alice came back from seeing Lily, she came to the shop where Syrena and I were working. She told us where she had been and why she had been there. Then she looked at Syrena and said, *Now, Syrena, you and I need to become friends. I am not your enemy. I know that you are in love with Luke, and I just want you to know that no one is pulling for you more than I am. It is true that I love Luke, but that is something that can never be. You and Luke are something that can be. I just ask your patience for the next*

*few months, because I will be seeing Luke some and asking his help with a project
I have in mind. Can you be patient, Syrena?"*

"Syrena answered, *I-I guess so, but I must admit, I don't understand.* That's
when Alice told both of us that she is dying. We all cried together. From
that day on, the two have been the best of friends. Syrena lives to make
Alice comfortable ... and they even talk about Luke sometimes."

"It's amazing," said Carrie. "I am so thankful that there is no animosity
or competition between them."

"Me, too, Maw!" exclaimed Belinda, giving her mother a big hug.
"Now let's go join the two new friends."

The four women had a wonderful afternoon together. When Cammy
woke up they all vied for her attention. Carrie smiled to herself all the way
home. At the supper table that night, she told Luke and Jessie about the
two new friends. Jessie was delighted, but Luke was a little perplexed.

"Maw," he said. "I have to take care of Alice the next few months. It's
what I need and want to do. How can I do that without hurting Syrena?
And, Maw, I don't even know how I feel about Syrena ... but I know I still
love Alice. This is just too confusing. Sometimes I don't know what I feel
about anything."

Carrie smiled. "I understand, Luke. Maybe you don't need to understand right now. Just go where God leads you. In time, you will know."

Alice sent word that she would like to see Luke on Saturday afternoon.
Nate was already there to see Carrie when Luke left.

"Are you worried, Carrie?" he asked.

"I don't know that I'm worried," she answered. "I am concerned,
though. I tell Luke to wait upon the Lord, but I don't seem to be able to
follow my own advice."

Nate took both her hands in his. "You're a mother, Carrie, and the
best I've ever seen. You're just acting like a mother."

With this, he took her in his arms and just held her ... and he had
never felt better in his life.

Luke arrived late that afternoon feeling nervous. Syrena met him at
the door.

"Hello, Luke," she said. "Alice is waiting for you in the sitting room.
Maybe I'll see you before you leave?"

Luke smiled weakly. "I'd like that, Syrena."

Alice looked the picture of serenity as he went into the sitting room. She was sitting on the sofa and motioned for him to join her.

"It's good to see you, Luke," she said. "Thank you for coming. I won't take too long, and then you need to take Syrena out for supper."

Luke just stared at her for a moment. Then he chose to ignore the last statement.

"You're looking good, Alice," he said. "Being back in Haymaker must agree with you."

She nodded. "I must say, this is the happiest and most content I've been in years. I'm glad I came back here. I just hope *you* won't come to regret it, Luke. Now, there is something I want you to do for me."

"Anything," answered Luke. "You just name it and I'll do it."

"It has to do with the money Mr. Ashton left me," said Alice. "I know what I want to do with it. Luke, I want to build an orphanage right here in Haymaker."

"An orphanage?" exclaimed Luke. "Why, Alice, I would never have thought of that, but it's a great idea."

"Do you think so?" she asked. "It's been on my mind ever since I found out about the inheritance. I want to do something good with it, and what could be better than a home for children who have been orphaned? But I want it to be a good home, Luke...not one like I grew up in. I want it to be a place of love, where children can feel they are important ... that they have a place to belong. And with the new school you're going to build, they could get a good education. It is so important that we find just the right people to run the orphanage ... people with hearts of love and compassion ... but people who can also be firm without being harsh."

"Sounds like you've been doing some thinking and planning," laughed Luke. "Now how can I help?"

"I want to tell you all my plans, Luke ... just how I want it to be. Then I will need you to get it done. Can you do that?"

Luke took her hand gently. "Of course. I can and will do it. How soon do you want to get started?"

"Well," she answered, "we both know I don't have a lot of time. I know I won't get to see it finished, but I would at least like to see it get started. Do you think that will be possible?"

"Absolutely," he assured her. "And who says you won't see it finished? You start writing down everything you envision it to be. Then Monday I'll come back by and we'll start drawing the plans. I believe we could get started within the next month ... maybe even sooner. How's that?"

"That's even more than I hoped for," Alice said. "And Luke, I want us to include the rest of the family in our planning. That includes Syrena and Mandy and Nate. Okay?"

Luke paused, then nodded. "Yes, Alice. If that's what you want."

"Then we are finished for now," she said. "Go get Syrena, take her out to supper, and fill her in on what we have talked about."

"Are you sure that's what you want?" questioned Luke. "You know I want to be with you."

"I'm tired and I intend to turn in early," she replied. "Now go get our plans underway and get Syrena's input on all of this."

So Luke and Syrena went to the diner, and he filled her in on Alice's vision for an orphanage. She sat and listened without interruption until he finished.

"We've got to do this for her, Luke," she said, "and we need to start right away. Wouldn't it be wonderful if she could see it finished? Do you think it's possible?"

Luke laughed in spite of himself. "I don't know who is more enthusiastic, you or Alice. I don't know if we can get it finished in time, Syrena. Only God knows that, but we can get busy right away. When I leave here I'm going to start asking around about carpenters. In the meantime, if Alice mentions an idea, write it down ... and write down your ideas also. Can you do that?"

"I most certainly can and will," said Syrena, eyes bright with assurance.

Over the weekend, Luke got some names of carpenters who were well-known and respected ... good at their trade and reliable. He intended to look them up and talk to them on Monday afternoon. Monday morning he went back to see Alice. She greeted him with a smile, but Luke noticed a paleness that had not been there before. He decided not to mention it.

"Good morning, Alice," he said. "Full of plans this morning?"

"Indeed I am," she laughed.

"I'll be talking with some carpenters this afternoon, so let's get to those plans," he said.

"Well, first of all," she began, "I would like for the caretakers of the orphanage to live *in* the orphanage. I don't want them living next door and leaving the care at night to hired workers. They need to be there every minute to know what's going on. We need a board of directors to make regulations and oversee the running of the place. I want you and Joe to be on the board of directors. Will you do that, Luke?"

"Yes," he replied, "and we can talk to Joe about it."

"Oh, I've already talked to him," she said smugly. "He said he would be honored. I don't know how many should be on the board, but I want the members to drop in quite frequently, and without notice, to check on things. I want them to talk with the orphans privately to see how they are doing and if they are happy and well-treated. Maybe that sounds overly cautious, but I know how my situation was, and I don't want that for anyone else."

"Your wish is my command," said Luke with a salute. "I think both ideas are good ones."

"I don't want it to be a big orphanage," she continued. "I think ten or twelve children would be a good number. That way they can receive more attention. They should have chores to do, but not become slaves. And, Luke, they must absolutely, positively be taken to church."

"Keep going," smiled Luke. "I'm listening."

Alice stopped to look at some notes she had written earlier. "I don't know where we can find land to build, Luke, but I hope it can be somewhere in or near town. I don't know if it will be possible, but if the land could be large enough for a garden, they could raise some of their own food, and that would help with the costs."

"I see you've been giving this a great deal of thought," said Luke, "and your ideas are excellent, Alice. Just don't wear yourself out with plans. We are all here for you."

"I know," she replied. "Actually, that last idea about the garden was Syrena's idea. It's a good one, though. Don't you think?"

Luke's cheeks reddened, but he nodded. "Yes, a very good one."

After talking just a while longer, Luke took his leave. He waved to Belinda and Syrena as he left, but did not take time to stop and chat.

By that afternoon, he had hired Zeb Williams and Bob Mueller to build the orphanage. He liked their zeal for their work and they had a reputation for honesty. Best of all, they could start as soon as the land was purchased and the plans were finalized. They even agreed to sit down with Luke and Alice to finalize the plans. Everything was coming together. Between the building of the school and the orphanage, Luke would be one busy man, but that was just what he needed.

That evening, after supper was over and he and Jessie had worked on the farm, they sat on the porch with Carrie, and Luke told them all about the plans.

"My biggest problem right now," said Luke, "is finding land for the orphanage. I'm figuring we need at least seven or eight acres. Jessie, have you heard of anyone who has land to sell?"

Jessie sat quietly for a minute. "No, I can't say that I have. But what if somebody had land to donate for the orphanage?"

"Donate?" asked Luke. "That would be better than good, but do you know anyone who would donate that much land?"

"I know a man who inherited a house and twenty acres of land," said Jessie, smiling. "That's about ten more acres than he will be needing. Would ten acres of land be enough for an orphanage?"

"Oh, great day!" shouted Luke. "I reckon it surely would."

"Like I've said so many times lately," laughed Carrie, "the Lord moves in mysterious ways. Who would have thought that Troy Ashton would leave you that land? And now it's going to be used for something that was dear to his heart. I'm certainly proud of you boys. You are both using your inheritance for something good. All you had to do was wait on the Lord."

"You know," said Jessie, "I was just thinking ... there's a section of the land that has apple trees, pear trees and cherry trees on it. They just need a little pruning. That would be a good food supply for the orphanage. Luke, why don't we go out there tomorrow and mark off ten good acres for it."

"I was just wondering," ventured Carrie, "do you have any imminent plans for the house and remaining ten acres, Jessie?"

Jessie's face became crimson. "I just might, Maw. I just might."

The following Sunday everyone came to Carrie's for dinner. The babies, Cammy and Ethan, received plenty of cuddling, and Leah and Nathan talked the men into a game of horseshoes. Later, while the children played or napped, all talk was about Cindy and her schooling, building the new school and the plans for the orphanage. Now that they had land, the plans were drawn up and the carpenters would begin building the orphanage in two weeks. The school, too, would soon be underway.

Alice sat quietly, listening to everyone talk. Luke noticed her quietness and her paleness. Looking over at Carrie, he could tell that she, too, noticed. Then he saw Syrena go over to sit next to her and saw them whispering.

"Miss Carrie," said Syrena, "Alice and I were just wondering if we might have a glass of your tea. You make the best tea in the world."

"Of course, you may," laughed Carrie, "and you don't have to butter me up to get it. Nate and I will go get the tea and glasses and we'll all have some."

With a few sips of tea, Alice seemed to regain some color. Before long, however, Belinda, Joe and Syrena announced it was time to go, and Alice left with them. Shortly after that, Ady Rose and her family left. Carrie, Nate, Luke, Jessie and Mandy sat on the porch and talked for awhile. Then Jessie rose from his chair.

"I think Mandy and I will go for a walk," he announced. "I haven't shown her where I grew up."

They walked out the path, passed the barn, and Jessie took her hand.

"Was it hard growing up here, Jessie?" she asked.

"Only some parts," answered Jessie. "It could all have been good had it not been for Paw. I'm scared to death of being like him, Mandy."

"Jessie, you are the kindest, sweetest, most gentle man I know," gasped Mandy. "Why would you ever think you would be like that?"

Jessie didn't answer and they continued to walk. Before long they were in the family cemetery. He led her over to two headstones. "This is where my Grandmother Cynthia and Grandpa Silas were buried. She died before I was born, so I never knew her, but people say she was a fine, generous, loving woman. She birthed a lot of the people in these parts. I was just little when Grandpa Silas died, but I remember him. He used to bounce me on his knee and tell me funny stories."

Mandy listened quietly, loving to hear Jessie talk about people she had never known. They walked over to a tiny headstone.

"This is where little Woody, my cousin, was buried," said Jessie. "He and Grandpa Silas died in the same house within minutes of each other. It was a sad time, from what Maw has told me."

Then they walked over to another grave.

"This is where Paw is buried," said Jessie, almost in a whisper. "I have to tell you about his death, Mandy."

Then Jessie told her everything that had happened the day of Tom's death. When he finished, they stood quietly together holding hands. Then Mandy put her arms around him.

"I'm so sorry you had to go through all of that," she said. "But one thing I know for sure, you could never kill anyone and you did not kill your paw. You've got to let it go, Jessie. Just the fact that you have been troubled about it all these years proves what a good, decent man you are. Can't you see that?"

Jessie stood in silence looking down at the grave.

"Am I the kind of man you could love?" he asked, without looking up.

She took his face in her hands and made him look at her.

"Oh, Jessie, don't you know? I already love you and have for a long time."

With this, he took her in his arms and kissed her.

"Am I the kind of man you could marry?" he asked.

"It depends," she answered. "Are you asking?"

With this, he went down on one knee. "Amanda Faller, would you marry me?"

Pulling him up, she exclaimed, "Yes, Jessie! Oh, yes, I will!"

Then he kissed her again. As they walked back down the hill and toward the house, he smiled. "You know, I haven't felt so good in a long time. Let's don't wait too long to get married. Okay?"

"Sounds good to me," she laughed. "Now, let's go tell Miss Carrie and Luke. Let's tell the whole world!"

"I don't think they'll be one bit surprised," said Jessie.

"Do you think they'll be happy?" asked Mandy, suddenly feeling a tad bit of fear. "Do you think they will want me in the family?"

Jessie laughed. "Mandy, I think they will be elated ... and breathe a sigh of relief. Some thought I would never marry. Of course, I thought that, too. Glad we were all wrong."

Hand in hand, they walked back toward the house, leaving the past behind and looking with great anticipation toward the future. They didn't know Carrie had been watching out the kitchen window, praying for their happiness, and praying for Jessie's peace. She knew from the way they walked and looked at each other that everything would be alright.

Thank you, Lord, she silently whispered.

CHAPTER 16

There was so much excitement in the Swank family that Sunday dinners were a bedlam, filled with noise from plans, and advice, and a great deal of kidding. Carrie loved every minute of it. She especially liked watching Nate. It seemed to be his own children who were making all the plans, and he was as excited as they were. He fit in quite nicely.

Okay, folks, listen up," said Jessie one Sunday. "If you want to hear the wedding plans, listen up."

"Oh, who's getting married?" teased Willy. "Anyone we know?"

"Very funny," said Jessie. "My brother-in-law, the comedian."

"Okay," said Carrie, "tell us. Tell us everything you have planned."

"We would like to be married the second week of December," said Jessie. "Cindy will be home for winter break. We will invite Clay and Abigail and hope they can come. All of you are invited ... except for maybe Willy."

They all laughed as Willy looked downcast.

"Where are you going to be married?" asked Belinda. "The hotel is available."

"We were hoping you would say that," said Mandy. "We would love to be married at the hotel. Nothing big. Mostly family. How does that sound?"

Everyone agreed that it was a splendid idea. Then the real plans began.

"What about a dress, Mandy?" asked Belinda.

"I don't want anything fancy," answered Mandy. "I do want a white dress, but something simple, and I was hoping...."

"Hoping what?" asked Belinda.

"I was hoping that you, Miss Carrie and Syrena would make my dress. It would make it so special."

"Gladly," said Belinda.

"We would love that," added Syrena. "Let's get together tomorrow and talk about what you want."

"We want to keep everything simple," continued Mandy. "No attendants, except I want you to be my matron of honor, Belinda."

"And I suppose I will have to let Luke be my best man," added Jessie.

"I'll have to ponder the matter," said Luke. "I'll see if I'm free that day."

This brought family laughter. Carrie looked over at Nate and smiled, a mixture of joy and contentment in her eyes. Nate took her hand in his, no longer afraid of what the children might think.

The date was set for Saturday, December 12, at 2 o'clock.

On Monday, the girls were gathered in the dress shop, discussing plans for Mandy's dress, as well as one for Belinda.

"I want a long dress, but nothing decorative," said Mandy. "Maybe a little lace on it. I don't want a veil. I want to wear flowers in my hair. What do you think?"

The women liked the idea.

"What color do you want my dress to be," Belinda asked Mandy.

Before Mandy could answer, they heard the hotel door open and then someone rang the desk bell. Belinda rose and started to the desk when a young man appeared in the doorway. He was in his mid-twenties, perhaps, with dark hair and a dark, well-trimmed mustache. Carrie stared at him, for he reminded her of someone.

He cleared his throat. "Excuse me, ladies. I don't mean to interrupt, but I didn't see anyone at the desk."

"Did you want a room?" asked Syrena.

"Well, yes, I do," he answered, "for me and my family. We just arrived on the train. I'm also looking for Alice Tyler, or, I mean Alice Warren."

Curiosity was in Alice's eyes as she looked at the stranger, and then she knew who he was.

"Homer?" she questioned. "Are you Homer ... my brother?"

"That I am!" he answered with the brightest smile she had ever seen. "It's been a long time, dear sister ... most of my life, in fact."

Alice rose and went to him. He opened his arms and she walked into them. They embraced, laughing and crying at the same time. The journey had been long, but at last brother and sister had found each other.

"Come in, Homer, and sit down," said Carrie, after a time. "I don't suppose you remember me, but I'm your aunt Carrie."

He immediately came to Carrie and embraced her. "I was just a baby when we were taken away. I don't remember much of anything or anyone, but Alice has told me a little about you and Aunt Nora and the day we were taken away. She told me you loved us enough to want to take us into your homes. It's good to meet you."

"Wait!" said Belinda. "You said you needed a room for you and your family. Where are they? We don't want to keep them waiting outside. You must have children, Homer. How many?"

Without answering, Homer left the room, returning with a woman and five children. The women looked at each other in amazement.

Seeing their bewilderment, Homer laughed. "This is my wife Trula. We have been married eight years. These are our sons ... Matthew, Mark, Luke and John. Not very original, I know, but befitting the sons of a minister. Trula is holding our little daughter, Martha."

They all hugged Trula and went from one to the other of the children, until the little ones were looking completely overwhelmed.

"Okay. Enough! Enough!" laughed Belinda. "We are confusing these poor little tykes.

Let's get you a room and let you get settled in. There will be plenty of time for getting to know each other. Are you sure one room will be enough?"

"Oh, certainly," answered Homer. "The kids are used to sleeping on the floor. We even brought additional blankets with us."

Belinda, who had finally introduced herself, Syrena and Mandy to them, led the way down the hall to a room. Carrie, Alice, Mandy and Syrena stood looking after them, shaking their heads.

"That's just like the Lord, Alice," said Carrie. "He takes away one and gives back seven. Now, Mandy, let's get back to those wedding plans."

They finished the plans and Mandy took her leave to go back to the mercantile that Luke had been watching after. She couldn't wait to tell him and Jessie about the latest development.

It was Sunday before they could all get together again, and this time seven more came for Sunday dinner. Carrie couldn't remember ever being so happy. Homer and his family fit right in, and it didn't take long to fall in love with all of them. Leah and Nathan were thrilled to have playmates. Alice even looked radiant with happiness. She finally had a family. After lunch they all adjourned to the front porch to talk and watch the children play. The three smallest were napping on Carrie's bed, tired from all the excitement, not to mention the cuddling each had received.

"Now," said Ady Rose, unable to wait a moment longer, "tell us all about yourself, Homer."

Homer, sitting next to Alice, reached over and took her hand. "It's been a long time since that day we were all taken away on the train. Fortunately, I don't remember that day at all. It must have been terrible for Alice, James, and even Belle. I was adopted within a few months by a wonderful couple who could have no children. My father was a minister in Ohio, and I was raised in a good God-fearing home with an abundance of love. Unfortunately, when I was sixteen, my father had a heart attack in the pulpit one Sunday morning and died within a few hours. My mother and I were left alone with very little money and no home. The house we had lived in belonged to the church, and though they allowed us to stay there six months, it eventually was needed for the new pastor. With the church's help, my mother got a job in a boarding house. She was paid very little, but we received a room and our food. She died when I was eighteen from overwork and a broken heart. I was then on my own."

"So, in a way, you were orphaned twice," whispered Ady Rose, wiping a tear.

"I guess you could look at it that way," said Homer, "but I, at least, had some wonderful, happy years. My adoptive parents taught me so much. I had to get a job immediately, but I knew where my heart was. I wanted to be a minister. I got a job in a factory, and that's where I met Trula. We were married six months later, and with her help, I went to school and became a minister ... two children later."

"Thank God for women like Trula," said Alice, patting her hand.

"Now tell them the best part, Homer," said Trula, nudging his arm.

"We are going to be staying in Haymaker," announced Homer.

This brought a round of applause and more hugs.

"This is more than I ever dreamed of," said Alice, unable to stop the tears.

"I was given a position as pastor at the little Missionary Baptist church on the outskirts of town," Homer continued. "The job doesn't, however, include a house, so we have to find somewhere for my clan to live."

"Does anyone know of a house for rent anywhere close?" asked Alice.

There was silence for a moment, then Jessie spoke. "Well, it's not very big and a little rundown, but Pete and Merl Jessup's house is empty. They went to Maryland to live with their daughter. I don't know if it's for rent or for sale, but I'll check on it."

"Oh, we'd be much obliged," said Trula. "Seven people in a hotel room is a little tight, even for us."

"There's one other thing I wanted to tell all of you," said Homer. "Tomorrow I'm going to see Lily. I don't know if she will want to see me, but this is something I have to do. I'll go by myself. Then, if she wants to meet Trula and the children, I'll take them later. If not, that's okay. I do want to make one thing clear, though ... I hold no hard feelings toward Lily. I forgave her long ago. My one desire now is to see her in church. That is my prayer ... and I believe it is my mission. I hope I will have everyone's support and prayers in this."

Homer was assured unanimously that they were behind him in his endeavor.

CHAPTER 17

Work was underway for both the new school and the orphanage. Luke made it a point to take Alice to the orphanage sight once a week, and each time she came up with new ideas. She was still feeling well at Thanksgiving and everyone came to Carrie's for Thanksgiving dinner, including Homer and his family. It was a special time in a family that deserved some special times. Homer, Trula and the children had moved into the Jessup homeplace two weeks before, but were looking for a larger place and one closer to town. Homer had begun pastoring his little church two Sundays ago and was happy with the job the Lord had given him.

As Jessie's and Mandy's wedding was only two weeks away, the talk of the afternoon focused on the wedding plans. The couple had been talking privately for quite some time to Homer. As they joined the rest of the family, Jessie cleared his throat.

"As you know," he said, "Brother Zeph has gone back to Willard County to be with his sister in her last days, and will not be able to officiate at our wedding. Therefore, Homer has agreed to marry the two of us."

"Yay!" they all shouted.

Carrie looked over at Nate and whispered, "The Lord moves in mysterious ways."

True to his word, Homer went to see Lily. As he knocked on her door, he felt no trepidation.

"Give me the words, Lord," he said aloud.

Lily opened the door, looking tired and worn. "Yes?" she said. "Is there something I can do for you?"

Without hesitation, Homer reached out his hand. "Hello, Lily. I'm your son Homer."

Lily was so shaken she grabbed for the door facing. Homer reached out to catch her, then helped her into the house and to the sofa.

"I guess I could have given a little more warning," laughed Homer, lightly. "Just take some deep breaths, Lily, and you'll be okay."

"Did you really say you are Homer?" she asked after a few minutes. "Are you really my son?"

"I most definitely am," he answered. "It is good to meet you, Lily. I've wondered about you for years ... what you would look like ... what you would sound like."

"You must hate me," said Lily. "I don't blame you. What I did was a horrible, selfish thing. I haven't lived a very good life, Homer, and I'm not a mother anyone could be proud of."

"No, Lily," Homer said. "I hold no anger or resentment toward you. Everyone makes mistakes in their life. We all sin, but the best part is that God loves us in spite of our mistakes."

"Do you really believe that?" she questioned.

"Well, I'd better," he laughed. "I'm a minister. What minister doesn't believe in the mercy and grace of God?"

"A minister!" gasped Lily. "My son is a minister?"

They talked for quite some time before Homer rose to take his leave.

"Lily," he said, taking her hand. "There is something I would like you to do for me."

She didn't speak, but her eyes held a question.

"I want you to come to my church this Sunday morning. Would you do that for me?"

Paling, she answered, "Homer, you don't want the likes of me in your church. The people will talk. It might hurt your ministry."

Continuing to hold her hand, he looked into her eyes. "Lily, I can honestly tell you, there is nothing I desire more than to see you in my church this Sunday morning ... with Dent, if he will come. Would you come, Lily?"

She slowly nodded. "Yes. I'll come."

Homer reached over and kissed her cheek. "I'll be looking for you."

As he took his leave, her hand went protectively to the place on her cheek where his kiss remained. She watched as he went out of the yard whistling. She couldn't, however, see the smile on his face, and as she closed the door, Homer gave a little skip.

"That skip is for you, Lord," he said.

Homer wasted no time in getting word to the rest of the family and asking them to come to his church on Sunday. Alice was the first to be told and the first to agree. One more prayer had been answered.

Sunday dawned cool, crisp and sunny. It was like the Good Lord had prepared the perfect day for them. One by one, the Swank family joined Homer, Trula and the kids at the church. The congregation welcomed them with friendly howdies, handshakes and hugs, and they all took their seats, waiting expectantly. About five minutes before the singing was to begin, the door opened, and as they looked around, Lily, then Dent, came shyly down the aisle. Nate tugged at Carrie's arm and she moved over, allowing room on the pew for her sister and brother-in-law. She smiled at Lily as they sat down. Homer preached a sermon on the prodigal son, and as he concluded his sermon, Carrie looked over and saw tears flooding Lily's wan cheeks. She reached over and took Lily's hand. Lily gave a little gasp and then smiled at her sister.

After the service, Homer stood at the door, speaking to each person as they left. When Lily reached the doorway, he motioned for Trula and the children to join him.

"Lily," he said, smiling, "I want you to meet my wife Trula ... and these are your grandchildren ... Matthew, Mark, Luke, John and Martha. Children, I want you to meet your grandmother."

Lily looked at them in amazement as they said in unison, "Hello, Grandma."

"And this," he said, taking Dent by the arm, "is Grandpa Dent."

This even brought tears to Dent's eyes. He and Lily left the church hand in hand, and watching them go, Carrie looked over at Nate.

"I know," Nate laughed. "The Lord moves in mysterious ways. And I must add, my dear, He always gets the job done."

As Alice walked out of the church, she turned to Homer and asked, "Do you think she will come back next Sunday?"

"I have no doubt whatsoever," answered Homer. "No doubt at all."

Cindy arrived home on December 9, just three days before the wedding. In her own bouncy, happy way, she told them all about school and entertained them with stories of her classmates. It was so good to hear her voice and see the "Mama Cynth smile". As they sat in the living room after supper one night, she asked,

"Luke, do you think I have a chance of getting a job at the new school? My grades are excellent and all of my teachers have assured me of a good recommendation. Is it too soon to submit an application? I want to teach, but oh, I do miss home."

"You just fix up that application and I will present it to the board," said Luke. "We plan to start looking at prospective teachers next week and I will highly recommend my little sister."

Jumping up to hug him, she said, "I do want to be back home. I feel like I'm missing out on everything."

"And we miss you," said Carrie. "We miss that energy and the happy smile. The most important thing we can do is pray about it."

December 12 tiptoed in with a cold temperature and sunny skies, but by noon those sunny skies were filling with clouds and tiny snowflakes were twinkling in the air. Nothing, however, would dampen the spirits of Jessie, Mandy and all the family. It was a day greatly anticipated. By one o'clock almost everyone had arrived, including Lily and Dent. Then the Swank family's dear friends Eliza and Turner Ashton and their three children arrived, along with Widow Thomas and Rollen. Eliza had helped Carrie through some tough times and loved the children as though they were her own. Clay and Abigail had sent regrets that they could not be there, as Abigail was expecting their baby any day now. Mr. and Mrs. Faller were unable to come, but had sent their best wishes, as had Mabel Ashton.

By two o'clock everyone was in place and ready. Trula played softly on the piano as Mandy walked into the room where Jessie, Belinda, Luke and Pastor Homer were waiting. Her eyes were shining with happiness and Jessie's were filled with adoration for this young woman with whom he intended to spend the rest of his life. He had never imagined he could have this much happiness, and he knew, without a doubt, that he would be good to his wife. He was not like Paw!

As the music ended, Homer began the ceremony.

"We are gathered here today to join this man and this woman in holy wedlock."

The ceremony continued and soon it was time for the ring.

"May I have the ring, please," said Homer.

Luke immediately removed the ring from his pocket and handed it to Homer, who then handed it to Jessie.

"Now repeat after me," said Homer. "With this ring...."

Jessie, holding the ring at the tip of her finger, repeated, "With this ring...."

"Owwww!"

The ceremony was interrupted with a loud squeal from little John who had just been pinched by his big brother Mark. The squeal scared Jessie and he dropped the ring. As he looked on in disbelief, the ring went rolling across the floor. The guests watched, too, some seeing the ring and others wondering what had just happened. Before anyone knew for sure what was going on, all the children were down in the floor trying to find the missing ring. As word was passed around, others joined in the search. Far from seeing the matter as a tragedy, everyone, including Mandy, was laughing as they searched. Only Jessie stood as though in a daze, perspiration running down into his collar, seeming unsure of what had happened. After about ten minutes of looking, a cry went up from young John.

"I dat it! I dat it!"

Sure enough, he was holding up the ring between his thumb and forefinger. His father took the ring from him with a reprimanding look. Joe collared Matthew and Mark and set them down next to him, while Willy gathered Luke and John, one in each hand, and set them down with his family. He nodded to Homer to carry on.

"Ahem!" said Homer, clearing his throat. "We will begin where we left off ... and may I remind certain young folks that God sees everything we do. He even knows when a sparrow falls."

At this, Carrie and Lily looked at each other and smiled, each remembering the time their brother Charles had killed a robin with his slingshot.

Charles, Papa Silas had said, *did I see a little bird lying dead under that sycamore tree last Thursday? It looked a might like it had been killed by a slingshot. Know anything about that?*

Y-yes, Papa, Charles had confessed, *I killed the bird. I-I'm sorry. I won't ever kill another bird as long as I live.*

And Papa Silas had said to him, *I believe you're a man of your word, Charles. Just remember, God knows even when a sparrow falls ... or a robin.*

It was almost as if Papa Silas was with them today and they could hear his voice once more. *He would have been proud of Homer,* thought Carrie, *and quite amused at his great-grandson.*

"With this ring, I thee wed," said Homer.

"I founded the ring!" said John loudly, looking up at his uncle Joe.

Joe nodded and put his finger to his lips, as everyone stifled their laughter. The ceremony continued.

"I now pronounce you man and wife," Homer was saying. "What God hath joined together, let no man put asunder. Jessie, you may kiss your bride."

As Jessie kissed Amanda, everyone applauded. It had been a ceremony to be long remembered and talked about at family gatherings. After a reception, the new couple took their leave, heading to their new home, the Ashton place, to begin their life. The guests soon dispersed, including Homer and his family who, no doubt, would be having a talk that night.

The following Friday night Nate came to see Carrie as usual. Cindy had tearfully returned to school and Luke was at the hotel, so they were alone. Carrie had fixed her special meatloaf and potatoes for Nate, ending with her molasses cake, and he enjoyed the meal immensely, never failing to brag on her food. As usual he helped her do the dishes ... drying as she washed. There was quiet between them, when all of a sudden Nate threw down the dish towel and turned Carrie to face him.

"Carrie, I've got something I gotta say, and I just can't wait any longer to say it."

She made no reply, but looked at him patiently.

"Carrie," he continued, "I don't have much to offer. I just have a little farm. Ain't worth much. But, well, here's the thing of it ... I love you,

Carrie. I have for a long, long time. I loved you as a person even when you were my sister-in-law. Now I don't mean that in a bad way. I just mean you were one of the best women I had ever known. But, Carrie, after Charlotte died, I came to love you as a woman, and I love you more and more every time I'm with you ... and the thing is, Carrie, I want to be with you all the time. I'll make you a good husband, and I'll be true and faithful. I'm not like Tom. I'll treasure you, Carrie, because ... because ... you are a treasure."

"Yes," said Carrie.

"What?" said Nate.

"Yes."

"Yes, what?"

"Yes, to the question you were going to ask."

"I was going to ask you to marry me."

"Yes."

"Yes, you will?"

"Yes, I will."

"You'll marry me?"

At this, Carrie burst out laughing. "Yes, my dear Nate, I will marry you. I love you, too, and have for a long time, although I was so afraid to admit it. I want to spend the rest of my life with you."

"You do?" he asked, as though he just couldn't grasp her words.

"Yes, Nate, I do," she laughed.

He stared at her for a moment in disbelief, and then pulled her into his arms and kissed her. He continued to hold her, not wanting to ever let her go, but finally released her and they finished the dishes, stopping every few minutes for another kiss. They even giggled like young folks and felt not one bit of shame.

Afterward, they retired to the living room where Nate just couldn't stop smiling.

"I practiced what I was going to say all week," he said. "I was determined to convince you, or die trying. Yet, in my heart, I was so afraid you would send me packing. Did you really say yes, Carrie?"

She snuggled close to him and whispered, "Yes, Nate. I said yes."

"Do we have to wait a long time?" he asked.

"Not unless you want to wait," answered Carrie.

"Then how soon?"

"Well, what would you say about one month from this Saturday?"

"Really? One month? Do you mean it?"

"Yes, I mean it," she laughed.

"One month from *this* Saturday?"

"Yes, just one month."

"Well, I'll be!" said Nate.

As he left that night, Carrie stood at the top of the steps, watching him leave. When he reached the bottom step, he turned and looked up at her.

"Did you really say yes?"

"I most certainly did," answered Carrie. "Good night, Nate." He ran back up the steps and kissed her. Then Nate went home ... smiling.

CHAPTER 18

Alice dreaded the task that lay before her. She talked with Homer about it one Sunday after church.

"Homer, I have to go see Lily, and I have to tell her that I'm dying. It wouldn't be right to put it off much longer and have her hear it from someone else. I just don't quite know how to do it."

"I will go with you, said Homer. "Would tomorrow be good for you?"

"You would really go with me?" asked Alice.

"Alice, we are a family," he replied. "That's what families do. They are there for each other. Of course I'll go with you."

With tearful eyes of gratitude, she hugged him. "Then let's do it tomorrow."

At ten o'clock the next morning, Homer met her at the hotel and they walked to Lily's house. The weather was crisp, but neither noticed, as their thoughts were on the task before them. Lily answered the door quickly after the knock, and for the first time she had a smile on her face.

"Come in out of the cold," she said. "What on earth are you doing out on such a cold day ... although I am glad to see you."

As she was speaking, Dent came into the room and shook hands with each of them. It was something he had not done before.

"I'm glad both of you are here," said Alice. "There's something I need to tell you."

Lily's bright face immediately paled. "What is it? I know something's wrong."

Alice went to the sofa and took her mother's hand. "I have to tell you the whole story of why I came back here. You see, I have been having some health problems, and when I went to the doctor he found something growing inside of me. He sent me to another doctor and I was given the same diagnosis."

"Oh, my!" exclaimed Lily. "Will you have to have surgery? Where will you have it?"

"No. No surgery," answered Alice, looking into Lily's eyes, willing her to understand.

Then, as Alice looked at her, the realization suddenly hit Lily.

"You're not saying...."

"Yes, Lily," said Alice, "I'm going to die."

"No! Don't say that!" yelled Lily. "I've just gotten to know you! I can't lose you! No! No!"

Homer went to sit on the other side of Lily. Dent sat across from them, eyes glistening with tears.

"Lily," said Homer, "I know this is a shock and it is hard. It is for me, too. I have just found my sister and soon I will have to say goodbye. But, Lily, this won't be the end. Alice is going to be in heaven and one day I'll be with her again. That's something we can all look forward to if we are saved."

"But why is God doing this to me?" asked Lily. "Is this my punishment?"

"No," he answered. "This is not a punishment. I do not claim to understand all that God does, but I know without a doubt, Lily, that God is a God of love and that His will is perfect. We just have to believe."

"I just don't understand why this is happening," said Lily, shaking her head.

"Neither do I, Lily," said Alice, "but I'm at peace with it, and I want to know that you are at peace with it, too."

"But how can I be at peace with losing my daughter when I'm just getting to know her?" asked Lily. "I don't know how to do that."

Homer held her hand. "Lily, I can tell you how, if you will let me."

She sat in silence as Homer told her about Jesus, and that He paid for all of our sins including hers. He told her of how she could one day see Alice again.

Then, with tears splashing on her dress, she nodded. "I want that, Homer. I truly do."

Coming over to kneel down in front of her, Dent said, "I want it too, Homer."

As Alice watched, she smiled with joy. If it took her death to bring this about, then it was all worthwhile.

Then Lily, as if suddenly remembering, asked, "Alice, how long?"

"Maybe a few more months," she answered. "Perhaps even more. I'm still feeling pretty well ... just tiring a little more easily."

"What are your plans?" asked Lily timidly. "I mean when the time ... draws ... near?"

"For now I'll remain at the hotel," answered Alice. "When I get to where I need help, Aunt Carrie has asked me to come stay with her, but I just can't do that ... because of Luke."

"Why not come here?" asked Lily, and Dent nodded.

"Oh, I couldn't do that," said Alice. "It will not be an easy thing."

Lily looked at her with pleading eyes. "Homer has just told me that God has forgiven my sins. Now let me be the mother I should have been years ago. Please, Alice. I need to do this ... for me as much as for you."

"I will help, too," said Dent, "just in case you're wondering how I feel about it. Let us take care of you, Alice."

Alice sat for a moment, just looking at them, thinking. "May I please pray about it?"

Homer took Alice's hand. "Alice, why don't we all pray about it right now?"

And that is what they did. And as they prayed, Alice knew. When the prayer ended, she looked at Lily and Dent, "Yes, I will most thankfully accept your offer ... but not until I believe the time is right. Can we agree to that?"

They all agreed, and Homer and Alice took their leave, with plans to see Lily and Dent in church on Sunday.

When they arrived back at the hotel, Belinda and Syrena could not believe the news.

"Are you sure about this, Alice?" asked Belinda.

"Yes, I'm sure," answered Alice. "I want my death to have some meaning, and this way it will. I can't be healed, but the lives of others who I love can be healed through my death."

"Then we are behind you all the way," said Belinda, hugging her.

"But that's a long ways off," said Syrena, "and we have work to do, ladies. So let's hop to it."

With laughter, that's just what they did.

On Sunday, Lily and Dent were at church, and afterward Carrie invited them to Sunday dinner with the rest of the family, which now, of course, included Homer's family. Christmas was just a few days away and everyone was filled with excitement, especially the children. Everyone agreed to gather at Carrie's. After dinner, as they sat around the table talking, Nate made his announcement.

"Luke, Belinda, Ady Rose, Jessie," he began, red-faced and nervous, "your mother and I have an announcement to make. Uh ... I have asked Carrie to marry me and she has said yes. I hope that meets with your approval because you are all as dear to me as if you were my own family ... and well ... we want to get married in three weeks."

Silence prevailed, but not before Carrie saw some twinkling eyes.

Clearing his throat, Luke said, "Well, what do you think, my dear siblings? Can we let this man marry our maw?"

"YES!!!" they all shouted together.

And right there in front of the whole bunch, Nate took Carrie in his arms and kissed her.

Then everybody hugged everybody. Even Lily and Dent joined in.

As Lily hugged her sister, she whispered, "I'm so happy for you, Carrie. No one deserves happiness more than you."

"Thank you, sister," replied Carrie, smiling.

Alice watched the two sisters. *Thank you, God. Lily will need Carrie when this is all over.*

Christmas was a joyous event, with happiness abounding, shadowed only by thoughts of Alice's health. She was feeling quite well, though, so those thoughts were set aside. Cindy had arrived back home for two weeks, intending to be there for her mother's wedding. It was a time for family and excitement and happiness. Two days before, Carrie had received a telegram from Clay with the news that Abigail had given birth to their son, Logan Isaac. Carrie now had five grandchildren!

"Do you think we'll ever get to see him, Maw?" asked Ady Rose.

Carrie's face clouded. "I can only hope, Ady Rose. I miss my youngest son and would love to meet his wife and my new grandson. I pray each night I will get to know them and hold my boy again."

The sadness in her face broke Nate's heart, and he reached to take her hand.

Feeling his hand of reassurance, Carrie added, "But right now, I have all of you with me, and I am happy and grateful."

The next few weeks were spent getting ready for the wedding. It would be a family affair, but Carrie and Nate both wanted to get married in Homer's church with Homer presiding over the ceremony. Eliza and her family, of course, would be invited. They just wanted to stand before their family and say their vows ... and that's what they did. Afterward, they went to the hotel for refreshments and everyone wished them well.

Here I am almost fifty years old, thought Carrie, as she watched her family mingle and laugh and chat. *Who would ever have thought I would find this much happiness again? Thank you, Lord, for Nate and for all of my loved ones.*

Suddenly Nate raised his hand and called above the din of voices.

"May I have your attention?"

The voices ceased and all eyes turned to Nate.

"I want to announce that my lovely bride and I will be leaving tomorrow morning and will be gone for one week."

Puzzled looks surrounded him ... but none more puzzled than Carrie's.

"I have a surprise for Carrie," he continued. "I have arranged for us to leave on the train at nine o'clock tomorrow morning to travel to Kentucky. We will be staying at a little inn just outside of Lexington, and yes ... we will be going to see Clay, Abigail and little Logan Isaac. I have already arranged it with them."

Gasps could be heard throughout the room, then wild applause.

"Really, Nate?" gasped Carrie. "Are we really going to see my son?"

"Yes, really, my love," he answered.

"Oh, Nate," she cried, not even trying to wipe the tears, "this is the greatest gift you could have given me."

The next morning they boarded the train, waving goodbye to their children with radiant, smiling faces.

Work on the orphanage was going even better than they had hoped. Dent had decided he wanted to help, so every day he went to the site. He helped in any way he could, whether it was holding boards in place while they were nailed or just sweeping up debris to keep the worksite clean. His volunteer work caught on and soon others in the community began to contribute whatever time they could spare. It became a community project, and nothing could have made Alice happier.

One day as she was sitting in the little dress shop sewing buttons on a dress for one of their customers, Homer and Trula came to see her.

"What a nice surprise," Alice said, looking up from her work. "I don't often see you two without the children. Who is taking care of them?"

"We left them for a little while with Lily and Dent," answered Trula. "Let's hope nothing is destroyed when we get back."

"I think that's wonderful," said Alice. "Lily and Dent need to get to know them."

Homer came to the sofa where Alice sat. "Trula and I have been praying and talking about something, Sis, and we decided it was time to bring it to you."

Alice's face showed alarm. "Oh, I hope nothing is wrong."

"No, no!" he answered. "I didn't mean to alarm you. It's just something we wanted to talk over with you. You see, the orphanage has come to mean a great deal to us. We know you need someone to live at the orphanage and take care of the children and the building and all. You need someone with a lot of love to give, and someone who can relate to the plight of those children ... and well, Alice ... we would like to be those people. We would like to be the caregivers and caretakers of the orphanage."

Alice sat in stunned silence.

"Alice, I know this is sudden," said Trula. "You will need to think about it. I know you might be afraid we can't handle it with our four little hooligans and their sister, and you probably wonder if we can give them the proper love, having our own and all. I assure you, we have prayed diligently about this, and we have plenty enough love to give. And we have patience, Alice. I think you can see that we have patience, and ... well...."

At this point, Trula ran out of words. She stopped, looking quite unsettled, as though there was more to say but she just didn't know what it was.

Alice still sat in silence.

"Alice?" said Homer. "Are you okay?"

Finally she looked up. "As Aunt Carrie always says ... God moves in mysterious ways. Just last night I knelt by my bed and asked God to send just the right people to run the orphanage ... and here you are. Yes! Yes! It would be an answer to my prayer to have the two of you run the orphanage, and I know you have plenty of love and understanding and patience to give. Thank you so much for taking this burden from me."

"We are glad to have your approval, Alice," said Homer, "but we also need to present it to Luke and Joe and the rest of the board to see if they will approve."

"I have no doubt about that at all," said Alice.

That evening when Luke came by the hotel, she told him the news. "Luke, I think they would be the perfect people for the orphanage. Don't you agree?"

"I definitely agree, Alice," he said. "Would Homer continue with his ministry in his church? I wouldn't want to see him give that up."

Alice nodded. "I agree. He would definitely keep his church. When he is away Trula would be there, as would other workers we will hire. We did agree, however, that either he or Trula would be there at all times, and if they both had to be away, they would take it before the board and make sure the children have proper care. I can't tell you how important that is to me."

"It sounds like everything is coming together," said Luke. "I can see the happiness in your eyes, but I also see fatigue. Are you feeling okay? You mustn't overdo it, you know. I know this is exciting, but please get your rest. I want you here as long as I can have you, my dear Alice."

She patted his hand. "And I want to be here as long as I can, Luke, but all of this is so important to me. I want to savor every moment of it. I do, however, think I'm going to have to cut down on my hours of work here in the shop. Maybe some of the time I can just sit here and watch Belinda and Syrena work. Nettie Willis has proven to be a tremendous help in the hotel, and Belinda is talking about hiring someone to help her, so Belinda can spend more time in the dress shop. I'm not sure how much Aunt Carrie will want to work now that she's a newlywed."

"I'm glad you're cutting back," said Luke. "You want to stay well enough for our weekly tours of the orphanage. It's coming along better than I ever expected, and the school will easily be finished for the next school year. I have some other news that I haven't told anyone yet, and you must be the soul of discretion."

"Absolutely," said Alice, her face showing excitement. "What is it?"

"The board has just approved Cindy for a teaching position," whispered Luke, all smiles.

"Oh my," gasped Alice. "Won't Aunt Carrie be happy!"

"We all will be," answered Luke. "I can't tell you how much I've missed my happy little sister. Now we have to fill the other three positions."

They talked for a little while longer until Luke saw the fatigue return to her eyes. He took his leave, promising to return the next day.

How can I be so happy and yet so sad? he asked himself as he went down the hotel steps. *It's like everything I'm working for just leads me one step closer to losing Alice.*

CHAPTER 19

Carrie and Nate returned from their honeymoon looking the picture of happiness. Nate would sell his house and little farm and they would live in Carrie's house, as that was her children's home. They agreed that Carrie would work one day a week at the dress shop unless she was needed more on special occasions. They had waited a long time for this happiness and they just wanted to be together.

Carrie brought back news of Clay, Abigail and little Logan Isaac. All of her quandaries about meeting Abigail had been washed away within minutes. She was a lovely, friendly young woman who obviously adored Clay. And Logan Isaac ... why, he was the most adorable little fellow she had ever seen ... along with Leah, Nathan, Cammy and Ethan, of course. She felt richly blessed.

"You should see the horse ranch where they live!" she exclaimed to her children. "It goes on for miles and miles! And Clay is so good with the horses. We watched him train them, and it is definitely his niche in life. Abigail's folks were nice, too. Not at all what I had expected ... which just goes to show that we should not judge. They made us feel welcome and even invited us to come stay with them the next time we visit. They even talked of all of them coming here when the baby is old enough to travel. Wouldn't that be something?"

"I think you can see that your mother is a little excited," laughed Nate.

"And very happy," she added, giving his arm a squeeze.

January wore into February, and with it came cold and snow, delaying work on the orphanage and school at times. Luke also had to face the fact that Alice's health was declining. She still sewed some, but oftentimes it was in her room. On those days, as often as possible, Syrena took her own sewing and joined Alice in her room. Alice told her, in her own words, about her life at the orphanage, about falling in love with Luke and how that was ruined. She also talked of her marriage. But most of all, she talked about the little girl she had loved more than life, but had lost. The two women, who loved the same man, became the best of friends.

It was mid-March and Carrie had been baking bread all morning while Nate went over to check on his farm. She was just putting the last pan in the oven when she heard a knock at the door. Wiping her hands on her apron, she opened the door to a wonderful surprise.

"Nora!" she squealed. "Oh, Nora!"

Then they were embracing. Two sisters who had always been so close and had always been there for each other, had not seen each other in almost two years. After Ben's death, Nora had gone to live with her daughter Leona. She and Carrie wrote to each other often, but letters could not take the place of their sisterly chats.

"What a surprise, Nora!" Carrie said. "Why didn't you tell me you were coming? Oh, it doesn't matter. You're here, and I am so glad to see you."

With this she gave Nora another hug.

"It's good to see you, sister," laughed Nora. "I didn't know we were coming until two days ago, but it was worth it just to see the surprise on your face. Oh, Carrie, it seems like it's been forever."

"How long can you stay?" asked Carrie. "Can you stay with us? There's plenty of room."

"Leona's Charlie got us rooms at the hotel," Nora replied. "We weren't sure until the last minute we were coming and we didn't want to put anyone out."

"Is anything wrong?" Carrie asked.

"Well, yes and no," said Nora. "The mine where Charlie worked shut down, so he is without a job. He received a letter the other day offering him a logging job up here, so if it works out, we'll be moving back here."

"Whoopee!" shouted Carrie. "I'll have my sister back. Oh, I pray it works out. Nora, tell me how you've been. I know losing that sweet Ben was devastating to you. He was such a good man."

"Yes," nodded Nora, "it's been hard. Leona and Charlie have been good to me, though. I've enjoyed living with them and their two children. They've made me feel wanted and at home. That's another reason we all came. If the job works out, we need to find a house to buy. They want me to continue living with them. Do you know of any houses for sale, Carrie?"

"Well, look who's here!" shouted a voice from the doorway.

Nate had just returned and was wreathed in smiles at seeing Nora.

"Hello, Nate," said Nora, rising from the sofa to embrace him. "I can see from my sister's happy eyes and rosy cheeks you have made her very happy, and no one deserves happiness more than she does."

"We are both happy," said Nate. "I love this woman more every day."

As they all sat down, Nate continued, "Did I hear you asking about a house for sale?"

"Yes," answered Nora. "I think we will be moving back here, and I sold mine and Ben's house when I left here, so we need a new home. Do you know of one?"

"Well, I might," he answered. "What did you have in mind?"

"We need a place big enough for Leona, Charlie, me and the two children," she replied. "We had talked about maybe a little farm where we can raise a garden and have a few animals, but I don't know if we will find all that we want."

"I don't know if it would be what you have in mind," ventured Nate, "but my house and little farm are for sale. The house is in good shape, but could use a little fixing up. It's plenty big enough, I think. I have forty acres of land with some good rich soil for a garden, and I even have two cows and two plow horses still over there. Jase Givens has been feeding them for me so I don't have to go back and forth every day. You're welcome to look at it, if you want."

Nora smiled. "I'm sure Charlie will be very interested, Nate. I can't wait to tell him."

"He don't need to feel any obligation, now," said Nate. "He can look at it and then decide if it fits all of your needs. No sense in buying a place you won't be happy in."

They ate lunch together and talked some more before Nora had to take her leave. She was anxious to tell Charlie and Leona about Nate's farm. That afternoon, Nate helped Carrie with some household chores as they talked with excitement about Nora's return and the possibility of selling Nate's farm.

"We can use the money to do some fixing up here," said Nate. "This could be a pretty good farm with a little work and a little money put into it. Would that be okay, Carrie? The farm would still be yours and then your kids' someday. I think of them as my kids, too."

"I know you do, Nate," she said, "and I'm so thankful for that. Maybe we could use a little of the money to go back and see Clay sometime. What do you think?"

"Whatever makes you happy, my love," he answered, pulling her to him. "I live to make you happy."

Two days later Nate took Charlie and Leona out to see the farm, and it was just what they wanted. Within two weeks, the papers were drawn up and the farm was sold, and in the bargain, Carrie got her sister back. She couldn't wait to begin their visits and their talks and just to catch up on the years behind them. She had told Nora all about the changes in Lily, and Nora wanted the two of them to go visit her one day soon.

All seemed bright and happy in Carrie's life except for Alice's illness and its ultimate outcome. Alice's health was failing more every time she saw her, and she knew that soon Alice would have to give up living in the hotel and go to live with Lily. She prayed that her last days would be peaceful ones and she and Lily would bridge the gap between them. They had come a long way, but the past was still there between them. Carrie knew that Homer would be there for Alice every step of the way, and he would be a great help to both Alice and Lily.

As she was pondering on these things one day, Nate came in with a letter in his hand.

"Guess who you got a letter from," he teased.

"Clay or Cindy?" she asked, grabbing for the letter.

"It would be from the lovely Cindy," he said, holding it high above his head. "It can be yours for just one kiss."

"Let me think about it," said Carrie, turning away.

"Hey, girl, is that any way to treat your man?" he laughed. With this he pulled her into his arms.

"Okay, okay!" she laughed. "You win."

And Nate got his kiss...two of them, in fact...maybe three.

Carrie sat down and opened the letter. As she read it aloud to Nate, her eyes got bigger and bigger. By the time she finished, they were both laughing and crying at the same time.

"We will save this for Sunday," said Carrie. "I want to read it to all the children at the same time. They are not going to believe this."

Sunday soon rolled around. Alice was not feeling well, so Homer and his family had dinner with Lily and Dent and then they went to see her. Nora, Leona, Charlie and their children came to Carrie's. Everyone was glad to see them and catch up on the years apart, and Leah and Nathan were glad to have two new playmates. After the dinner was over, they all gathered around the fireplace in the living room as the little ones played a game in the dining room. Carrie pulled Cindy's letter from her apron pocket.

"I have a letter here from your baby sister," she announced. "I thought while we're all together I would read it to you."

"I'll bet she's anxious to come home," said Ady Rose. "I'm so thankful she was approved for the teaching position. Things just aren't the same around here without our cheerful Cindy."

"Okay, Maw," said Jessie, holding Mandy's hand. "Read it to us.

Carrie opened the letter and began....

Dear Maw,

It's snowy and white here today. In fact, it has been for the past two weeks. I love snow, but I sure would like to see the ground again. I hope all of you are doing well. Give my siblings and dear Nate my love, and tell them I'll be seeing them soon. Can you believe I only have two months left here? It has been a wonderful year in many ways. I have learned so much and can't wait to get in the classroom and put some of my ideas into use.

That brings me to another subject. Maw, do you remember all the times I told you I never wanted to marry? All I wanted to do was teach school? Well, Maw, I've met someone ... a young man ... who also wants to be a teacher. We have so much in common. Sometimes we just talk for hours and hours. He's really good looking, although looks are not the important thing, as you have always told me, Maw. His name is Landon McLindy. Isn't that a beautiful name? He wants to teach what they call here "high school." That's all the grades above seventh grade. He is really good at math, which is not my easiest subject, so he helps me sometimes with my teaching projects on math. He has so many good ideas for making it interesting for the children. I don't want you to get the wrong idea, Maw. He hasn't proposed or anything. He doesn't even have a job yet, although he has sent out several applications, including one to the school at Haymaker. Don't tell Luke because I don't want him to think I'm asking for favors. Landon wants to get the job on his own merit. That's how special he is. Like I said, Maw, he hasn't proposed ... but, Maw, if he ever does, I think I would say yes. Does that surprise you? It does me a little, because I never once figured on marriage. I thought my heart belonged to the classroom, but, Maw, can't your heart belong to two places? Marrying Landon wouldn't change the way I feel about teaching. Oh, I wish you were here right now so we could talk and you could give me your wonderful advice.

I wonder what my brothers and sisters are going to think of all this. I told them so many times marriage was not for me. Do you think they'll understand? Oh, I know they will. They've always wanted me to be happy. I wish all of you could meet Landon. I know you would love him.

I'll just add this. It will make you laugh, Maw, and you're so beautiful when you laugh. If I marry Landon McLindy ... my name will be Cindy McLindy. Isn't that a hoot, Maw?

I must close now and get ready for class. I think of you every single day, Maw, and look forward to the time I can be back home. Give everyone my love ... and pray for me and any decisions I have to make.

Your loving daughter,
Cindy

By the time Carrie finished the letter they were all bouncing with laughter.

"Cindy McLindy!" shouted Jessie. "Only our Cindy could come up with that."

"It will be so good to have her back home," laughed Belinda.

"You know," said Luke, looking a little more serious. "We did go over an application the other day from a Landon McLindy, and all the board members were impressed. If I remember right, he was an orphan who was adopted by a banker and his wife. His father has since died and he has only his widowed mother."

"Wow!" exclaimed Ady Rose. "What a coincidence!"

"Do you think he will get the job?" asked Carrie.

"I believe he has already been approved," answered Luke, "but don't tell Cindy. That's for him to find out first."

"Well," said Nate, "we may all be meeting Landon McLindy even sooner than Cindy had hoped. As you always say, Carrie,

"The Lord moves in mysterious ways!" they all chorused.

They all talked on awhile about Cindy, about Lily and Dent, and about Alice. It was only then Luke's eyes took on their sad look, and Carrie could see that he, also, was living in dread of what would ultimately come. Her heart ached for him, but also for Syrena, who could not help but know what this was doing to him. Carrie admired the girl's loyalty to him in spite of his love for another, but she also admired her for the love and kindness she showed to Alice.

Before Nora left, she and Carrie made plans to go see Lily the following week.

CHAPTER 20

April would soon be blossoming, and the days were becoming a little longer and a little sunnier. It was on one of these late March days of sunshine that the two sisters made their way to Haymaker to visit Lily. The dread Carrie would once have felt was no longer there.

Lily greeted them with a smile. "It's good to see you both. Nora, I heard that you had moved back and I'm glad. We've all missed out on a lot of each other's lives, mostly because of my ways, but maybe we can catch up now. Dent and I are going to my son's church now. I hope you will join us there. Who would ever have imagined the likes of me would have a son who is a minister?"

Nora laughed. "I plan to be there next Sunday, along with the rest of my family. Carrie has told me all about Homer and his family, and I can't wait to meet them."

"Lily, how is Alice?" asked Carrie, quietly.

Lily just shook her head. "Not well. Not well at all. My heart just aches for that girl, but she's got more spunk than anyone I've ever known. Right now, Carrie, I think that orphanage is keeping her alive."

"She does have a heart for that orphanage," said Carrie. "Do you think she'll still be coming here to stay?"

"Yes," answered Lily, "and I don't think it will be long now. Just pray for me, girls, that I can be the mother I never was before. I want to be there for her, but not smother her. Pray that I can do that."

"You'll do just fine, Lily," said Carrie with confidence. "We will be praying for you both."

The sisters took their leave, and from there went to the hotel to see Alice. Carrie could not believe the change just a few days had made. Dark circles surrounded her eyes. She did not rise as they came into her room, but her smile told them she was glad to have them visit.

"Aunt Carrie and Aunt Nora," she said. "My two favorite aunts. Nora it is so good to have you back here. I'll bet you are glad to see the happiness in Aunt Carrie's eyes, and isn't that Nate just a darling? His eyes dance every time he looks at her."

"Yes, they do," laughed Nora. "I have noticed. Everyone notices. How are you, Alice?"

"I'm doing okay," said Alice. "There's no use to try to hide what is obvious. I know my health is failing, but I've already done better than the doctors expected. I'm beginning to believe I might just live to see the orphanage finished. Wouldn't that be grand?"

"It would, indeed," said Carrie, "and I believe you will."

Alice looked down at her hands for a few moments. "Aunt Carrie, I think I will be going to stay with Lily soon. Do you think I'm doing the right thing? This will not be easy for her. Do you think she realizes how difficult this will be, and do you think she is up to it?"

"Yes, my dear," answered Carrie. "I think she realizes to the extent that anyone can who has never experienced it."

"I don't want to be a burden to anyone," said Alice. "I couldn't stand to think I was a burden. I worry about Luke, too. Do you think he will be able to handle this? I want so much for him to be happy. I want him to see what a special woman Syrena is. Do you think he will see that?"

"Alice, there are some things I can't answer," said Carrie, taking her hand. "Some things only God knows, but I do believe Luke will be okay ... maybe not for awhile ... but he will be okay. God will take care of him, I have no doubt."

"Then I can die in peace," said Alice, "knowing that the people I love most in the world will be alright. You take good care of him, Aunt Carrie ... and Lily, too."

The two sisters visited a short time with Belinda, Cammy and Syrena and then headed home. It had been a day of happiness and sadness at the same time ... but such was life.

The following weekend Luke picked Alice up at the hotel and drove her, with all of her belongings, to Lily's house. Belinda and Syrena used all the strength they could muster to hold back the tears. Syrena promised to stop by several days a week with hand sewing for Alice to do, and with a heavy heart, Luke drove away.

Lily and Dent welcomed her with open arms and hearts of love. Dent had brought a small bed into the living room where she could lie down and rest during the day when she was tired. They also fixed her a special chair near the window with a table beside it for her sewing and her Bible. They had prepared for her comfort as well as they knew how. Luke knew that she would be well taken care of, but he also knew this was where she would die. He vowed to himself that he would stop by every day, and that he would be there for her and remain strong every step of the way. Life must be all about Alice in the time that remained.

The orphanage was almost finished, and the school would be ready by June, in plenty of time before school was to begin. Luke visited the orphan-age site every day, making sure the progress was coming along as quickly as was possible. It had to be completed for Alice to see. It just had to be.

On Sundays Homer and his family had begun going to Lily's after church for Sunday dinner. Alice was unable to go to church, so most Sundays Lily stayed home with her. Some Sundays Syrena showed up and insisted Lily go with Dent to church and give Syrena and Alice some "girl time." On these days, she read to Alice from the Bible and they prayed together. Then Syrena caught Alice up on all the doings at the hotel. They had formed a special bond. When Lily, Dent, Homer and the others returned, Syrena left to have dinner at Carrie's.

It was on one of these Sundays at Carrie's that Belinda and Joe made an unexpected announcement. Dinner was over and they had settled in the living room. The days were becoming warmer, but it was still a bit chilly for sitting on the front porch.

"Ahem!" said Joe, drawing everyone's attention. "My lovely wife and I have an announcement to make, and being the kind, loving husband that I am, I will let her tell you our news."

Belinda was smiling and her eyes were glowing.

"Well..." she began, "we're going to have a baby!"

Everyone squealed and applauded at the same time.

"Will you be getting it from the same orphanage Cammy came from?" asked Ady Rose.

"How old is it?" asked Willy.

"No, no!" said Belinda, shaking her head. "You didn't hear what I said. I'm going to have a baby!"

They all sat in stunned silence.

"You mean?" said her mother.

"Yes, Mama. I'm pregnant!

With the realization, tears came streaming down Carrie's cheeks, and she went straight to her oldest daughter ... the daughter she had almost lost twice in her childhood. As she held her, the past came swirling back into her memory ... the memory of the days when Belinda had lain lifeless in her bed, so close to death.

"Oh, my daughter," she said. "My heart rejoices for you. Thank God for his wonderful love and mercy."

Luke was next in line to hug her. He, too, remembered those times he had sat by her bed, willing her to wake up. He remembered the joy in his heart when she had awakened and he had told her how long she had been asleep. She wouldn't believe him until her mother had confirmed it. He remembered the walks they had taken to help get her strength back.

Thank you, God, his heart spoke. *Thank you for bringing me back here, if just for this very moment.*

"When is it due?" asked the pragmatic Ady Rose. "How long have you known?"

"Well," responded Belinda, "I have known for sure for three days, but I have suspected for a few weeks. I was just afraid to hope. Syrena knew, but I was afraid even to tell Joe, because I didn't want to get his hopes up and then disappoint him."

Joe took her in his arms. "My darling, you could never disappoint me. You are the light of my life."

Smiling the smile of an expectant mother, Belinda continued, "As for when ... I am already five months along, so it should arrive in early August."

"Five months!" shouted Ady Rose. "You are five months pregnant and didn't know it?"

"Well," laughed Belinda, "I've never been pregnant before. I haven't been one bit sick."

"Not sick!" exclaimed Ady Rose. "You are one lucky girl."

The baby that would soon join their family monopolized the conversation the rest of the afternoon. It was only after everyone else left that Luke talked to his mother and Nate.

"Maw, Alice is getting much worse. I don't know how long she has left, but I'm afraid it won't be long. The orphanage will be finished by mid-week. I am planning a little dedication ceremony next Saturday at the orphanage. I want to have it while Alice can still be there. There will be a few words of dedication, then Homer will read some scripture and have a prayer. After that, the sign will go up, designating the name of the orphanage. When that is done, there will be a tour of the facility and refreshments. Do you think you could make some cakes and pies, Maw?"

"Absolutely," answered Carrie. "I am glad you asked me. Luke, will you be able to handle all of this?"

"I have to, Maw," he said. "This is for Alice."

Saturday dawned sunny and warm, as if God was granting them a special day for the orphanage dedication. Carrie and Nate began the day on their knees by their bedside, asking God to grant Alice a happy day and to give Luke the strength he would need.

Luke drove to Lily's to get her, Dent and Alice and take them to the dedication. Alice was so weak he carried her to the car. He had borrowed a wheelchair to use when they got there. She had been unable to go to the site for a few weeks and her eyes lit up when it came in view.

"Oh, Luke," she gasped. "I can't believe it's finished. My dream has actually come true."

Luke retrieved the wheelchair from the trunk and helped her into it. Lily placed a blanket around her shoulders to keep out any chill, and then they moved her to the front where a temporary podium had been set up. At exactly eleven o'clock, Luke called for quiet.

"I would like to welcome all of you who have come out for this special occasion. As you can see, our orphanage is finished. It has long been the dream of Alice Tyler Warren, and today that dream is a realization. Let's all give Alice a hand."

With this there was thunderous applause and whistling.

"We will be able to house ten children in the facility," continued Luke, "and Alice doesn't know this yet, but we are to receive the first two children next month."

This brought more applause and whistling. Alice's eyes sparkled.

"I see this orphanage as something for the entire community," Luke went on. "It is a place where we can show love to children who need it, and I invite all of you to volunteer your time and talents. Homer and Trula Riteman, brother and sister-in-law of Alice, will be living on the premises and running the orphanage along with their five children. As most of you know, Homer is the pastor of Haymaker Missionary Baptist Church. Also ... and this is a surprise for Alice ... her mother, Lily Tyler, will be the cook for this facility ... and her step-father, Dent Tyler, will be the janitor and handyman."

This brought more applause and a gasp from Alice, as she turned to look at Lily and Dent.

"Really?" she asked.

"Absolutely," answered Lily, and she and Dent were both shedding happy tears.

"It is my hope," continued Luke, "that some of you ladies will volunteer some time to help Lily in the kitchen and you men to help Dent with the groundwork. We have hired two other ladies, Mavis Couch and Gracie Moore, to do laundry and housework. The children living at the orphanage will attend our new school if they are of school age ... and they will all attend church on Sunday. If any of you ladies sew, maybe you can make clothes for the children. If any of you quilt, perhaps you might contribute quilts. There's plenty for each of us to do. Let's all take an active part in our orphanage."

After a few more remarks, Luke turned the podium over to Homer. Then it was time for the unveiling of the name.

"It is time to name our new orphanage," said Luke. "Willy, Jessie, Joe ... would you help me, please?"

130

The young men went up to the front where a sign was covered with a cloth. As they removed the covering, everyone gasped, but no one as loudly as Alice.

Luke beamed. "Our new orphanage, ladies and gentlemen ... Alice's Hope.

By this time everyone was either applauding, laughing or crying. Luke wheeled Alice up closer to see the sign, which would later be placed on the front of the building. She could hardly see it through the tears, as she reached out to brush her frail hand across it.

"Oh, Luke," she cried. "Oh, Luke. How can I thank you, my darling, my love?"

"The joy in your eyes is more thanks than I will ever need," said Luke, kneeling in front of her. "All of this is due to you, my dear Alice. It was your dream and your hope that you put into action. Many orphans will owe a happy life to you."

With this, he took her in his arms and held her, not caring at all who saw.

Alice was tiring, and after going inside briefly, they packed some refreshments, and Luke took her and Dent and Lily home. Her dream had been fulfilled. Now Luke dreaded what lay ahead.

CHAPTER 21

Syrena kept her word and went by to see Alice almost daily. Alice could no longer sew, but Syrena would take her own work and sew as the two women talked.

"What do you think heaven will be like?" asked Alice, as they sat together one sunny day. She had been looking out the window quietly for some time.

"I don't think we can even imagine," answered Syrena, continuing to sew. "But I do know that it will be beautiful. I don't think we have words here on earth that could adequately describe it."

"I will hate to leave all of you," continued Alice, "but I am actually looking forward to it, Syrena. I will see my little girl again."

"Yes, you most definitely will."

"Syrena," said Alice, looking away from the window and into her friend's face, "I want you to be there for Luke. Will you promise me that?"

Syrena stopped sewing and looked at Alice. "I will if he will let me, Alice, but I'm not sure he will allow me to be a part of his life. I love him. You know that I do, but I can't make him love me. Yet, I will be there."

"That's all I can ask," said Alice. "You've been a true friend … no, more like a sister. I'm not sure I could have done for you what you have done for me. I love you, Syrena."

"And I love you, Alice," she said. "I will always be thankful I met you and we had this time together. You've taught me to appreciate life and to be compassionate to others."

The next day Belinda stopped by to see Alice. She was showing now with her pregnancy, and she almost glowed with happiness.

"Come over here," said Alice, as Belinda came in. "Kneel down here."

Belinda did as she asked, and Alice placed her hand on Belinda's stomach and just sat quietly for a moment.

"It's going to be a boy, Belinda," she said finally. "You're going to have a beautiful little blonde-haired boy."

Belinda looked at Alice, somehow knowing that her words were true. "Thank you, Alice, for telling me that. Cammy will love having a brother."

She left a short time later, smiling at the memory of Alice's words. A little boy! She decided it would be her and Alice's secret. Wouldn't Joe be surprised!

In the middle of May, Cindy returned home ... with Landon. The family immediately fell in love with the young man. He was everything Cindy had said he was, and Carrie knew he would soon be her son-in-law. He and Nate hit it off from the beginning. Landon turned down their offer to stay at their house, and instead, rented a room at the hotel until something permanent became available.

"It just wouldn't be appropriate for me to stay at Cindy's home," he said, "especially with both of us being teachers and all. No use to cause talk if you can avoid it. Besides, my mother will be coming soon and I will get her a room at the hotel also."

Landon's mother, he told them, was all alone now. She had no family left, and was looking forward to moving to Haymaker. She had already met Cindy and, like everyone else who knew Cindy, fell in love with her at their first meeting.

"If your mother needs a place to stay," offered Carrie, "she is welcome to stay here. It would save her money."

"Thank you, Miss Carrie," he replied. "Actually my mother has talked about building a boarding house here for people who might be staying permanently and cannot afford to remain a long time at the hotel. We are not wealthy by any means, but my father left her some money, and she feels that would be a good investment. A boarding house would even be good for teachers like myself who need a place to live. I don't mean to sound like I'm boasting, but my mother would be the perfect person to run a boarding house. You'll see what I mean when you meet her."

Nate nodded. "I think that's a wonderful idea, Landon. The men who built the orphanage are excellent carpenters. She might want to talk to them when she arrives."

"There's something else we wanted to talk to the two of you about," said Landon, taking Cindy by the hand. "I'm sure it comes as no surprise that I am in love with Cindy, and she loves me. I would like to marry her, but it is very important that we have your blessing."

"Cindy has always been a good judge of character," said Carrie. "We already care for you, Landon, and I can see the love in your eyes for my daughter. You have our blessing. Right, Nate?"

Nate nodded. "Just take good care of our girl, Landon. She is one of a kind."

"Oh, I definitely know that, sir," agreed Landon, the love showing in his eyes as he looked into Cindy's."

"When were you thinking of having the wedding," asked Carrie. "You know Alice is very ill now. It won't be long."

"We talked about that, Maw," said Cindy. "Because of that, I don't want a big wedding. Do you think it would be appropriate to just gather at Homer's church with the family and have a quiet ceremony? That way, we wouldn't have to do a lot of planning, and if we had to postpone it, we could do it at a moment's notice. We just want to be married before school starts in the fall, and we hope to live at Mother McLindy's boarding house when it is finished ... at least until we decide to build a home of our own. What do you think?"

"Oh, my darling Cindy," said Carrie. "You've always had such a good head on your shoulders and you've always thought of others. You are one lucky man, Landon McLindy."

Alice continued to weaken. Her days and nights now were spent in bed and she ate very little. Lily sat by her constantly, telling her stories of her own childhood ... stories of Mama Cynth and Papa Silas. She had never really known these people, but they came alive through Lily's stories. She was amazed when Lily told her that Mama Cynth had birthed over two hundred babies in her lifetime.

"She truly had a God-given gift," whispered Alice.

"Oh, yes," agreed Lily, "but we girls didn't think of it as a gift when she had to be gone for two or three days. We got downright mad sometimes."

Alice laughed weakly. Then she suddenly thought of something. "Did Mama Cynth birth me, Lily?"

"She sure did, honey!" laughed Alice. "She said I was loud enough for ten women while I was in labor."

At this time they were interrupted by a knock at the door.

"I'll bet you have a visitor," said Lily, making her way to the door. "I've never seen anyone have so many friends. Well, come in, Luke. I know Alice will be glad to see you."

Luke walked over to the little bed and looked down at the woman he loved. She was little more than a shell now, but still beautiful. He could see how weak she was, but as she looked up at him, the smile in her heart crept up and tugged at her lips just enough to form a perceptible smile.

"Hi, Alice," he said. "Have you and Lily behaved yourself today?"

"We'll never tell, will we, honey?" laughed Lily. "Now, you two sit and talk and I'll go make some tea. Maybe you can even coax her into eating a little, Luke."

"Do you hurt anywhere, Alice?" he asked quietly, after Lily had left. "Are you nauseous? Is that why you can't eat?"

"I don't hurt," she answered weakly. "Just no appetite."

"Can I do anything?" he asked.

"Just sit here beside me," she said, reaching out with the little strength she had to take his hand. "Luke, there are some things I want to say to you and this might be the last chance I have. No. Don't say anything. We both know it will be soon."

Unbidden tears came into his eyes.

"Luke, I can die happy if I know you will be happy," she said. "Syrena loves you, and I think, if you let yourself, you can love her. I want you to let yourself love her. She is a special, special woman, and I have come to love her as a sister. Don't live in the past, Luke. The past is gone. Look to the future. There's happiness out there if you will just reach out and grasp it. Please, Luke, promise me you will try."

Luke looked at her for a long time, trying to speak past the wrenching, tearing pain in his chest. "I will try, Alice. That's all I can promise. I will try."

The hint of a smile returned to her face. "Now tell me the latest news about the orphanage, the school and anything else you know."

Luke stayed awhile longer, telling her about Cindy and Landon and their plans to marry. He also told her about the plans for a boarding house, and she loved the idea. As he talked on, Alice fell asleep. He tucked the covers around her shoulders and kissed her on the cheek.

"Goodnight, my beautiful Alice," he whispered.

CHAPTER 22

A few days later, Sarah McLindy blew into town like a whirlwind. She had requested that Carrie and Nate join Cindy and Landon in meeting her at the train station. No sooner had the train come to a halt than a little round lady with rosy cheeks stood at the top step, waiting to disembark.

"Yoo-hoo!" she called, waving a lacy, white handkerchief. "I'm here!"

As the conductor helped her down from the train, Landon made his way to her, followed by the others. Carrie couldn't help but think of a female Santa when she looked at Mrs. McLindy.

"Oh, it is so good to be here," she trilled. "Oh, Landon, it is good to see you ... and Cindy, dear, give me a hug. My, you get more beautiful every time I see you. And this must be Carrie and Nate. I do hope I can call you that, and you must call me Sarah. It was so nice of you to come meet me. I hope it wasn't an inconvenience, but I just couldn't wait to meet Cindy's parents. I do love that girl of yours, you know."

By this time, Carrie wanted to help Sarah McLindy take a breath.

"Mother, slow down," laughed Landon.

"Oh, I know," laughed Sarah. "I do go on. But I'm so excited. I couldn't wait to meet everyone and to see the little town where I am going to live. A new beginning!"

Carrie walked over and took her by the hand. "We are excited to meet you, too, Sarah. Your son has told us so much about you."

"Oh, I bet he told you what a chatter box I am," said Sarah. "I just enjoy life and getting to know people. Now, here, we're going to be family, so give me a hug. Landon, dear, would you fetch my bags, please. I'm afraid there are several of them."

As they all looked back toward the train, the conductor was wiping his forehead with his red bandana handkerchief as he carried bag after bag and placed them in a stack. Landon, Cindy, Carrie and Nate looked at each other and broke into laughter. Then Sarah joined them.

"I know I could have sent it earlier," she said, "but I just like my belongings with me."

Nate and Landon went to load her luggage onto the wagon they had brought. Cindy and Carrie ushered Sarah over to a bench in the shade as they waited.

"I hope I'm not being a bother," said Sarah, fanning her face with her white, lace hanky.

"Absolutely not," replied Carrie. "We are just glad you are here. I know we are going to be good friends, Sarah. You are like a breath of sunshine."

"Well, we have much to do," said Sarah. "We have to get these young folks married and then I have to build my boarding house. Do you think the boarding house is a good idea, Carrie? I plan to have nice rooms for my guests, and I can cook for them. Oh, I do love to cook and make pies and cakes...."

"I'm sure people will flock to your boarding house," laughed Carrie, "and I can't wait to taste one of your pies or cakes."

Sarah brushed back a strand of white hair that had escaped from the tight little bun in the back. "I'll need your help and your input, and I do hope you will help me get to know the folks in the community. I just know I'm going to love it here. The reverend always said, "Make people happy and you will be happy.""

"The reverend?" questioned Carrie.

"My husband," smiled Sarah, as though seeing his face. "The late Reverend Jonathan McLindy, God rest his soul. A fine man he was, and I miss him terribly. Okay, enough of that. This is a happy day! Now off to the hotel with me. I'm anxious to meet Belinda and I'm sure we are going to become good friends. I hear she's with child. Oh, glory be!"

As they were all loaded with the bags, the group made their way to the hotel. Carrie was anxious to see the look on Belinda and Syrena's faces when they met this jovial lady. No doubt, Haymaker Hotel would never be the same!

After they deposited Sarah McLindy at the hotel, with Landon to entertain her, Carrie, Nate and Cindy made their way home, full of conversation about their day.

"I know she's bouncy and never runs out of things to say," laughed Cindy, "but I do love her. She has so much love and joy in her. It kind of gets contagious after you are with her awhile. Maybe she's just what we need around here."

"I think you are definitely right," agreed Carrie. "One can't stay glum and sad around her for long. I think she will be good for our family and even for our community, and I'm certainly happy she loves my daughter so much."

"Could we just ride in silence for a few minutes?" asked Nate, looking a little worn. "My ears are hurting."

This brought gales of laughter from Carrie and Cindy ... and a little smile from Nate.

Sarah didn't let any grass grow under her feet, so to speak. Within two days of arriving in Haymaker, she had hired the two men who had built the orphanage to build her boarding house, promising not only to pay the salary they asked, but to bake them pies and cakes while they worked. She was also in the process of closing a deal on land for her boarding house right in Haymaker. It seemed no one could resist the jolly Sarah. While at the hotel, she insisted on helping with the chores of cleaning rooms, doing the wash and anything else she saw to do. Belinda and Syrena were completely taken with her.

On Sunday, she came to dinner at Carrie's with the rest of the family, minus Alice and Homer and his family, who would be eating with Lily and Dent. Soon Sarah had won the hearts of the entire Swank family, especially the little ones. They took to her right away when she pulled stick candy from her dress pocket.

Nathan looked at Sarah as he licked his candy, curiosity obvious in his eyes. Finally he walked up to her and put his free hand on hers.

"Do you know Santa Claus?" he asked, eyes wide.

"Why, I surely do, child," she answered, bobbing her head up and down. "He's one of my dearest friends."

"Wow!" said Nathan, and with that, he just walked away, leaving everyone in muffled laughter.

Luke stood aside from the others in the living room, just watching Sarah McLindy, a thought slowly taking place in his mind. Eventually, when everyone else was occupied, he walked over to her chair.

"Mrs. McLindy, could I talk to you for just a minute?"

"Why, certainly, child," she answered. "I can tell you have something on your mind. Now how can I help you?"

Hesitating only a moment, Luke said, "I suppose you know about Alice."

"Well, yes," she said. "Cindy and Landon told me a bit and then Belinda told me more about her only yesterday. She sounds like a delightful person, and yesterday afternoon I went over to see the orphanage. You know that homes for orphans have a special place in my heart. That's how we got our dear Landon. The reverend and I wanted a child so badly, and God was saving just the right one for us. But I'm going on again. Tell me what you need, dear Luke."

"I've been watching you," he said. "You seem so happy and cheerful and I think you might be good for Alice right now. She doesn't have much time left with us, I'm afraid. Mrs. McLindy, do you think you might go see Alice? I think meeting you and talking with you would be good for her."

"Why, child, I can't think of anything I would like better," Sarah said. "I'll scoot right on over there tomorrow morning. I want to meet Lily, too. I think she and I could be friends."

True to her word, the next morning Sarah made her way to Lily's house, carrying a butterscotch pie in her hand and humming *Amazing Grace* as she walked along. After a quick little rap on the door, it opened and Lily stood there perplexed.

"Good morning to you," Sarah greeted her, smiling. "You must be Lily. I am Sarah McLindy, the mother of Landon McLindy. You know he's engaged to Cindy Swank, I suppose. Well, I've only been in town for a few days, but

I wanted to meet you and visit with that sweet Alice of yours. I brought you one of my butterscotch pies. Now you just go cut yourself a piece and pour yourself a tall glass of milk and relax yourself while I visit for a few moments with your daughter. Could you show me the way?"

Unable to utter a word, Lily led her to Alice's room.

"Thank you, dear," whispered Sarah. "I promise I won't stay long, and then you and I can have a little visit."

With this, Sarah walked quietly into Alice's room and looked down at the pale face of a lovely young woman. *Sweet father*, she whispered in her heart, *let me bring some joy to this little soul here before me*. Then she went over and opened the curtains ever so slightly.

Alice blinked as the light touched her eyes.

"Is that too much light, dearie?" whispered Sarah.

"No," Alice answered faintly. "Wh-who are you?"

Keeping her voice low and gentle, Sarah answered, "I am Sarah McLindy. My son Landon is to marry your cousin Cindy Swank. I've heard all about you, Alice, and I wanted to come meet you. The reverend always said, "Don't be putting off things. Just put your foot out there and go."

"The reverend?" asked Alice. "Am I dreaming?"

"No, darling," laughed Sarah. "I tend to rattle sometimes. The reverend was my late husband. He was a minister of the gospel and I just always called him by that. I talked to Luke yesterday and he told me all about you, Alice, and I just couldn't wait to meet you. May I place a pillow behind your head and maybe help you sit up a bit?"

"That would be good," replied Alice. "I'm a little weak, I guess."

Sarah proceeded to fluff a pillow, raise Alice gently and put the pillow under her head. Color seemed to flow into Alice's cheeks as Sarah continued talking.

"I went by to see your orphanage, and oh, I do love it! It will make a fine, happy home for those without parents. I suppose you know that our Landon was adopted. He has been such a joy to my life. You have done a great thing, Alice, in building that orphanage, and you can just bet I'll be sharing my pies and cakes with them quite often."

"Oh, Mrs. McLindy," gasped Alice, "that will be just magnificent. I want the orphanage to be a success. I suppose you know that I grew up in an orphanage ... not a very nice one ... and I want this to be a happy home for those left orphaned."

"I just know it will be," said Sarah, patting Alice's hand. "Now, what about you, dear? How are you feeling?"

Alice smiled. "Suddenly I feel ... lighter. I know that's a strange word to use, but it seems to fit. It's like you brought some sunshine into my room with you."

Sarah laughed. "Nothing like a little sunshine to lift the spirits! At least that was the reverend's way of thinking, and he was a wise man. Now could we talk about you, dear? Tell me what is on your mind."

"Oh, I guess a lot of things," Alice replied. "When you don't have long left, you tend to think about all kinds of things, and you want to make sure you cover all that needs to be covered in your last days. Mrs. McLindy, you said your husband was a minister. Did he talk much about heaven? Did he ever say what it will be like?"

"Why, yes, dear. He often talked about heaven and how beautiful it will be ... no more sadness, no more sickness. Can you imagine never seeing anyone sick anymore? Why, that will be just wonderful! He said it will be a beautiful place and everyone will be happy. Oh, I know he is so happy up there. He was always a jolly person ... never said an unkind word about anyone. I miss him so, but I know he's bringing even more happiness to those already there."

"I'm not afraid of dying," said Alice. "I just wonder about it."

"Of course you do," soothed Sarah. "We all do, but your days here are not over yet. You just enjoy every minute with those who love you. I know your life has not been an easy one, but you have brought love to so many people. It is quite obvious how that handsome Luke feels about you. I know the story, Alice, and it's a sad one...but it's also a special one. Some people go through a whole lifetime and never know that kind of love. So, you see, you are quite blessed."

"Thank you, Mrs. McLindy," said Alice. "I guess I've never taken time to think of it that way. I've always looked at it as something I lost, but I haven't really lost it, have I? Just because it can never be doesn't mean it is lost. I like that. Thank you for helping me to see that."

"It's my pleasure, sweetie. Now I must scoot out of here before I wear you out, and besides, I want to get to know your mother before I leave. Maybe I can come back in a few days and we can talk some more."

Alice smiled again. "I would truly like that. Please do. Would you ask Lily to bring me a little tea? I think I could drink some now."

With this, Sarah McLindy took her leave, as Alice lay smiling. "Thank you, God," Sarah whispered.

She made her way into the living room where Lily sat waiting. Sarah delivered the message about the tea and then sat quietly while Lily took it in to Alice. When she returned, Sarah smiled up at her.

"Sit with me a moment, Lily. I would like to get to know you."

Lily sat down, still perplexed by Sarah McLindy.

"I don't know what you said to Alice," remarked Lily, "but I haven't seen her look so happy in days. Thank you, Mrs. McLindy."

"It's *Sarah*, dear," she replied. "Please call me Sarah, and I hope I can call you Lily. I feel that we are going to be good friends. I intend to be bringing lots of my pies and cakes over to the orphanage when the children get here."

"Your pie was delicious," said Lily, "and it would be wonderful to have them for the children. I'm going to be preparing the meals, you know, and I will welcome all the help I can get. Sarah, I suppose you know the story behind Alice and how I gave my children away. Are you sure you want to be friends with someone who would do all that?"

"Dear heart," said Sarah soothingly, "we all make mistakes. None of us are perfect. Just look at what you are doing now. It is obvious you are sorry and you are doing something about it. No one can do more than that. Now, you have to forgive yourself, so you can move on. God has great things in store for you, Lily."

"You really think so?" asked Lily, her face showing surprise.

"Absolutely," declared Sarah. "You can count on it ... and you can always count on God."

Sarah soon took her leave, heading back to the hotel in high spirits. She had much to do in her life and she planned to enjoy every minute. She looked around the little town of Haymaker as she walked along. A new school...a new orphanage...and soon a new boarding house. The little town was growing and she would enjoy spending the rest of her days here, until she could go see the reverend.

Sarah continued to visit Alice often, bringing sunshine with her as she came. Four children had arrived at the orphanage, and she regaled Alice with her description of each one.

"Oh, you should see little Henry ... only four years old, but he has the most laughing eyes, and I'm sure he's just full of mischief. When he arrived they found a frog in his pocket and he would not give it up. So Homer and Trula made it a home and Henry named him *Mr. Frog.* Now everyone watches their step over there, if you know what I mean!"

As weak as she was, Alice laughed out loud at this story.

Sarah continued. "Little Hazel is five years old and sharp as a tack, but rather shy. She has the brightest blue eyes and blonde hair so curly both ends meet. And then there's Ralphy. He's only two and a sad little boy, but I'm sure in no time Henry will have him talking and laughing. The oldest is Lissa, all of six years old, and a little mother to the others. She gets up every morning, makes her bed and then heads to the kitchen asking to help. Oh, I do hope they will find homes, as they would make any family happy."

"Thank you, Sarah," said Alice, smiling. "You make my day happy when you come and tell me about the children. I always look forward to your next visit, wondering what story you will have to tell."

But even Sarah had to admit Alice was failing. The little spark was gone from her eyes and she found it more and more difficult to talk. Yet, she loved Sarah's visits ... but Lily seemed to love them even more. She had found her first true friend. They laughed, talked and shared recipes. It was something Lily had never known before. Sarah even helped her to understand as Alice weakened.

"Darling," soothed Sarah, "it is something we all must face. It is not easy losing our loved ones and it will never be, but it is a part of life. You will see Alice again one day. Of that, you can rest assured, just like I will see my dear Jonathan again."

"I don't think too many people would understand this," said Lily, "but maybe you will. These last days have been wonderful for me. I know that sounds strange, but I have been given a second chance to make some memories with my daughter. I lost all of her first years, but God gave me these last days with her, and it has meant so much to me."

A week later as Carrie, Nate and Luke were finishing supper, there was a knock at the door. Nate answered to see Dent standing before him. Dent nodded to Nate, then looked beyond him to see Luke coming to the door.

"Luke," said Dent, eyes filled with tears, "Lily says you better come."

That's all he had to say. Knowing what lay ahead, Luke kissed Carrie and whispered, "Pray for me, Maw."

The men traveled back to Haymaker in silence, each knowing, yet not wanting to know.

As Luke entered Alice's room, Lily sat beside her bed. She shook her head and rose to give Luke her chair. She and Dent stepped outside the room so they could have their privacy. Lily patted Luke's shoulder as she left.

Luke sat down and took Alice's hand gently in his. "Alice, I'm here," he whispered.

She stirred ever so slightly. "Luke," she said, almost inaudibly.

"Yes, my darling," he replied. "I'm right here beside you."

She didn't say anymore, but her face showed peace at knowing of his presence. He began to talk to her.

"I remember the first time I saw you, Alice. I thought you were the most beautiful creature I had ever seen. Then as I came to know you, I realized as beautiful as you were on the outside, it didn't even compare to the beauty on the inside. Remember, what fun we had fixing up the house we bought? The snowball bush is so big now."

He paused for a moment to make sure she was still breathing, then continued,

"The orphanage was such a grand idea, my love. The children are happy there and Homer and Trula are just the perfect ones to run the place. They have an abundance of love and patience. The entire community is helping. Can you believe that, Alice? You have brought an entire community together."

With this, Luke just couldn't go on. He could not get the words to take voice. He watched her shallow breathing as dread clutched at his throat until he thought he would die. But then, he wanted to die ... oh, the blessed release. Luke watched death take over her body, inch by inch, his world slipping away. As he held her hand, Alice gave two little gasps, and then she was gone. The hand he held went limp, as tears flowed from his eyes.

"Good-bye, my dearest," he whispered.

Seeming to know what had happened, Lily and Dent came into the room. As Dent pulled the sheet over Alice, Lily sank to the floor crying. Luke sat down in the floor next to her and held her as they mourned their loss together.

Two days later, Alice was buried in the little family cemetery atop the hill where Papa Silas and Mama Cynth had been laid to rest. The entire community came out to say goodbye to this brave young woman who had won their hearts.

"To everything there is a season," read Homer, in a voice as strong as he could muster, "a time to be born and a time to die."

"My sister lived her life to bring joy to others," he continued, "and in that, she was more than successful. In the short time we were together, she brought unspeakable joy to my life. I am so thankful I was able to know her."

As the graveside service ended, everyone walked back down the hill. Only Luke remained. He sat on the ground beside her grave ... remembering. He remembered the good things, and as he did so, he let go of the bad.

"Thank you, God," he whispered. "I thank you that I had her in my life. The happiness far outweighed the heartache."

Then, as Luke arose, like dew settling gently on the grass, a peace settled over him. God still had a purpose for him, and he was ready. He turned to make his way back down the hill, and as he did, he caught sight of movement just a ways off. As his eyes focused, he saw that it was Syrena, and as he walked toward her, she reached out her hand to him. He took her hand in his and forbade himself to look back. The future lay ahead and he knew, whatever that future held for him, he had found a place to belong.

In July, Cindy and Landon were married.

In August, Belinda gave birth to a beautiful, blue-eyed, blonde-haired little boy.

In December, Jessie and Mandy welcomed a little boy into the world.

Carrie and Nate still sit on the front porch and hold hands ... and Nate smiles.

A COUNTRY BOY
FINDS PEACE

The years have not been easy,
But he knows he is most blessed.
His heart aches with sadness
As he lays his love to rest.

Their love was never meant to be.
It was not in God's plan.
But God still has a purpose
For this lonely, searching man.

This is where he is meant to be,
And this is where he'll stay.
Today has its fill of sorrow,
But tomorrow is another day.

So he will look to the future,
And God will make him strong,
For he has found a reason to live,
And now a place to belong.

– Brenda Crissman Musick

ABOUT THE AUTHOR

Brenda Crissman Musick grew up in the hills of Appalachia and loves it with a love only a product of the area can truly realize. "I can't imagine living anywhere else," she says. "I love the friendliness, the loyalty, natural beauty and the front porch mind frame."

Her childhood days were spent outside, running barefoot in the summer and building snowmen and making "snow cream" in the winter. She loved using her imagination to create games, stories and songs. Brenda has been writing stories for as long as she can remember, taking them to school and forcing her classmates to read them. She wrote poems of love to her husband while he was serving his country in Vietnam.

Brenda taught elementary and middle school in the Russell County School System...some of the most rewarding years of her life...her desire always to instill a joy of learning in her students. "I will never be bored as long as there is a book in the world," she often told them. She loves genealogy research, compiling family histories for her children, hoping they, too, will always appreciate their heritage. As an outlet for her desire to teach, she teaches Bible Studies for adults at her church. "A writer must write and a teacher must teach," she says.

In 2000, Brenda published a children's book, *The Dolls on the Old Stairway*. She has taught classes on Creative Writing to both students and teachers, and in 2013 she taught Memoir Writing at the Appalachian Heritage Writers' Symposium at SWCC. In the fall of 2013, she fulfilled her dream of writing a novel with *One-Eyed Tom*. There was more of the story to tell, however, and this novel, *A Place to Belong*, is a continuation of the story.

Brenda and her husband Jimmie enjoy "retired" life on a small farm in the Big A Mountain section of Honaker, a beautiful, peaceful place, with the best of neighbors. They have three children and seven gorgeous grandchildren, thirteen cows and a bull named Ralph.

Contact Brenda at: musickb@jetbroadband.com, facebook.com/Brenda Crissman Musick, or by mail at P.O. Box 344, Honaker, VA 24260.

COMING SOON

PON MY HONOR,
STORIES AND POEMS FROM
THE COUNTRY SIDE OF LIFE

This is a compilation of stories and poems from
the life of the author as well as stories she says were
"buzzing around in her head." She tells about the day
her brother and his friends came toting a dead skunk
through their kitchen...or the days of early telephones,
wringer washers and outhouses....and Old Charlie,
her grandfather's horse that didn't like little girls.

ALSO

TO EVERYTHING
THERE IS A SEASON

...sequel to
ONE-EYED TOM and
A PLACE TO BELONG
The Swank family's story must continue.